# Mesopotamian Mythology

Classic stories from the Sumerian Mythology, Akkadian Mythology, Babylonian Mythology and Assyrian Mythology

## (Classical Mythology Book 7)

*By Scott Lewis*

# Table of Contents

# Introduction

The ancient culture of Mesopotamia once thrived along the banks of the Euphrates and Tigris Rivers in what is modern-day Iraq, Syria, and Kuwait. Often called the Fertile Crescent, this region teemed with ancient civilizations that achieved mind-boggling levels of the socio-economic and political organization and technological advances. The cultures of the Sumerians, Akkadians, Babylonians, and Assyrians dominated the region and developed agrarian societies that gave rise to the first cities in the world.

These ancient cultures established themselves around 4,000 BCE with the rise of the Sumerian Empire. With the establishment of societies, a rich mythology formed around their pantheon of gods. Across the region, their religions overlapped and developed over 1,000 different deities. The lore of the ancient Mesopotamian societies focused on the gods and their interactions with one another and mankind. The early civilizations created myths and stories to explain why and how things happened. It is fascinating to delve into their histories and see how they explained their universe.

Interestingly, this area was populated by several societies that remained independent of each other, but their gods and religious practices overlapped. They never unified under a central rule like other civilizations of the time, including the ancient Egyptians. Trade existed among them, and inevitably, war broke out from time to time. However, for the most part, they remained separate nations. These ancient people were extremely advanced for their time, and their belief systems were intricate and complex.

Luckily, the Sumerians developed a written language to record their legends, myths, and lore. It started with a picture system, much like hieroglyphics, and evolved into a complex writing system, called cuneiform writing. These writings, chiseled into clay tablets, preserved the stories, but unfortunately, as the ancient civilizations declined, the tablets did not typically survived intact. Archeologists and historians recover and restore the tablets as they are discovered. Translation can be difficult because the tablets resemble giant jigsaw puzzles with pieces missing and text that has been eroded over time. Regardless, these precious written records have given us a solid idea of ancient Mesopotamian beliefs, lives, and culture.

Through the extensive archeological work done in Mesopotamia, we have a fairly realistic picture of what life in that time and place looked like. Before we get into the mythology of the era, let us first look at the different civilizations that existed in Mesopotamia. With that understanding, we will then explore the creation myths of the region. Finally, we will cover the most popular mythological stories of the time, including the Epic of Gilgamesh in its entirety.

# Chapter 1 Who Were the People of Ancient Mesopotamia?

Four main cultures existed in ancient Mesopotamia. There were several other smaller tribes scattered throughout the area as well, but these main four established cities and a unified culture. The oldest of these societies were the Sumerians.

The origin of the Sumerians, like many ancient people, is not completely clear. However, in their literature, they mention their homeland to be Dilmun. Dilmun is believed to be an island in the Persian Gulf, most likely the modern-day island of Bahrain. On the banks of the Euphrates River, the Sumerians settled and built the first city of Eridu somewhere around 5500 BCE. In their records, they referred to themselves as the black-headed people, and they had just built the first organized settlement in the world. They had made the first shift from a hunter-gatherer existence to an agrarian society that built an infrastructure and worked to cultivate both animals and crops.

While Eridu was the first settlement, Uruk is usually acknowledged as the first city in the world. It was initially ruled by priests who reigned from the temples. The citizens were basically slaves to the temple who worked tirelessly to create enough offerings to the gods to win their favors. Eventually, the priests gave way to kings. The first recorded king in the Sumerian Empire was Etana of Kish. The Sumerians were ruled by a monarchy that was advised by a council of elders, on which both men and women served.

The Sumerian Empire existed until it was finally conquered by the Amorites and Elamites around 1750 BCE. While they existed, they reached amazing technological advances. The oldest known wheel is credited to the Sumerians, and they made ornate temples, statues, and pottery. Their infrastructure included roads and irrigation systems, and their cities were protected by walls. They also created the sailboat and were leaders in improving weapons from stone to copper to bronze. The cities thrived, and an economy was established.

Culturally, they developed a moral code and judicial system to enforce it. The Sumerians also invented a numeric system and a structure to monitor time. They based their time measurements on the number 60 and marked the passage of time down to seconds. The Sumerians even established an average length of a workday and the 24-hour clock.

The Sumerians also traded with other early civilizations. There is evidence of contact and possible trade between them and the ancient Egyptians. The Sumerian Empire grew and prospered, and so did some of the surrounding societies. Mainly, the city-states of Sumer traded among themselves and lived peaceably for centuries. The odd war broke out between tribes over irrigation and land rights, but overall, there was a long period of stability in the region.

Around 2300 BCE, a second culture established itself in Mesopotamia. The Akkadians, centered in the city of Akkad, developed their own language that soon became the most commonly spoken language in the region. The Sumerian language was gradually relegated to religious and official dialects, much like Latin was in Medieval Europe. Sargon, a gardener in the palace of King Ur-Zababa, led a coup against the king and usurped the throne. Under his reign, the Akkadians began several centuries of domination of the area.

Sargon believed that all of Mesopotamia should be unified under one rule—his. He led a bloody campaign through the river valleys until Sumerians bowed to him. Beyond conquering surrounding cultures, Sargon opened trade routes throughout the region and into Egypt using their surplus grains and agricultural products to bring in precious metals and ore.

The monarchy traveled down through Sargon's descendants. Each king's reign typically lasted a couple of decades, and most of it was spent in suppressing insurrections in the various city-states within the empire. The kings declared they were the kings of the "four corners of the Universe," and one of the final kings, Naram-Sin, actually signed his name with a symbol that put him on the same level as the gods.

History would later remember Naram-Sin in a story that blamed him for the fall of the Akkadian Empire. According to the Curse of Agade, Naram-Sin lost the favor of the god Enlil, God of the Fates. The reason for the loss of favor is unsure, but possibly because Naram-Sin was much occupied with conquests and warfare and not with the worship of his god. Enlil withdrew his blessing from Naram-Sin, and the king beseeched Enlil to tell him why. He prayed and made offerings, but Enlil had turned his back on the monarch. Not only had Enlil turned away, but all of the other gods had also been banned from showing favor to the Akkadians. After seven long years of pleading and depression over their fate, Naram-Sin had had enough. He rallied his army and destroyed Enlil's temple in the city. This, of course, angered Enlil and the other gods even more, and they sent the Gutians to destroy the Akkadians. This is not a historically accurate tale of Naram-Sin's reign, but it does illustrate the trend of the time to use the kings in literature to tell a story and send a message.

The Akkadian rule was brief and unsettled. A short two centuries after it was established, it had fallen to the Gutians, a barbarian tribe that crossed the Zagros Mountains and conquered the river valleys. This invasion ushered in a dark, chaotic time with no political organization in the Mesopotamian region.

Historians have found evidence that while the Gutians conquered the Akkadians, there was likely a widespread famine in the area at the time. Evidence of a profound drought has been discovered that suggests the Akkadians were in a very vulnerable state, and the Gutians took advantage of it.

Eventually, the dark ages came to a close with the re-establishment of another Sumerian monarchy, and order was slowly restored to the area. This era was short-lived due to the migration of the Amorites, a people from the northern reaches of Mesopotamia. As they spread across the southern third of what had once been the Sumerian Empire, they wrestled control from the Sumerians. They also established new cities, most notably, Babylon. The First Babylonian Empire had just begun.

Around 1894 BCE, Babylon was a town of little importance and was mainly dominated by the Elamites, another strong Mesopotamian society. Eventually, Hammurabi came to power and really put Babylon on the map. Hammurabi was a skilled leader and marshaled the government into one central entity, set up a tax system, and firmly brought all the surrounding territory to heel under his rule.

Hammurabi was not content with just ruling the city of Babylon. He dreamed of expanding his empire. With a vast, well-disciplined army, Hammurabi built the Babylonian Empire that covered the central and southern portions of Mesopotamia. Babylon was designated as the holy city, and there was a shift in the principle deity from Enlil to Marduk. Several of the other ancient Mesopotamian gods slipped from their dominance in the pantheon, and a new set of gods and goddesses took their place. Trade thrived, and there was a time of prosperity and stability. It disintegrated after Hammurabi's death, and the Babylonian Empire was ruled by several different tribes. The Kassites ruled for over 500 years and kept Babylon as the center of religious power. The Hittites and the Elamites also ruled for different periods of time. No matter who ruled the region, they all had one main problem—the Assyrians.

The Assyrians had inhabited the northern third of Mesopotamia since the first Sumerian rule. They had been swallowed by the Sumerian and Akkadian empires temporarily over the years only to regain their independence as those empires rose and fell. The unified Assyrian Empire was established around 1900 BCE with the construction of the city of Ashur, named for their chief deity. The Assyrians initially used Akkadian as their language but adopted Aramaic as their national tongue soon after they came together as a society. Their culture was highly organized, much like the other ancient Mesopotamian cultures. However, their customs appear to be a bit harsher and less gender equal than their southern cousins. The texts found from their judicial proceedings include routine executions, beatings, and whippings. Men definitely had far more rights than women, but there were harsh penalties for sexual assaults. There was required military service from all young men which helps explain their ready military resources to withstand the multiple invasion attempts throughout the years.

The Assyrians were skilled ironworkers and had firm ties to Egypt. These influenced their ability to defend their territory, and as they grew stronger as an empire, they expanded and conquered neighboring empires. During the Middle Assyrian Empire, they sought to expand throughout Mesopotamia and adopted a unique way of dealing with the people they conquered. After they sacked an area, they deported the native inhabitants and replaced them with Assyrian families. As barbaric as the custom sounds, records show that the Assyrians were very methodical about keeping deported families together and sending people to places where their talents were needed.

Around 1240 BCE, King Tukulti-Ninurta came to power, succeeding his father who had just decimated the neighboring tribe, the Mitanni. Tukulti-Ninurta focused on amassing knowledge from the people they conquered and for a while, was a very popular king. However, the Babylonians were once again stirring along the Assyrian borders, and in retaliation to the Babylonian threat, Tukulti-Ninurta sacked the city of Babylon, destroying the sacred temple, and enslaving a large portion of the population. The Assyrian people took offense to the desecration of the sacred structure, and they turned against their king, assassinating him.

There was another dark age in Mesopotamia called the Bronze Age Collapse when chaos reigned throughout the area. The Assyrian Empire dwindled but maintained a firm control on the heart of their territory. They also maintained open trade routes and re-established themselves faster than their neighboring societies. As soon as they were once again well-established and thriving, the Assyrians began to expand their holdings. Under the rule of Tiglath-Pileser III, the Assyrian Empire overran the entire region, reaching its pinnacle. Tiglath-Pileser III was responsible for making radical changes to the administration of the government and military, as well as economic and political systems. He has been credited for laying the foundations for the Greek, Persian, Turkish, and Roman governments.

One of the greatest Assyrian kings, Ashurbanipal, was a scholar who spoke, read, and wrote multiple languages. He was a humanitarian and sent supplies to neighboring cultures during times of famine and hardship. Conversely, he was known to be a ruthless warrior and showed little mercy to his enemies. Probably his largest accomplishment was the amassing of the cuneiform tablets in the great library at Nineveh, where he had moved his court. It was considered a sacred duty for kings to compile knowledge, but Ashurbanipal was obsessed with the concept. His goal was to compile all of the knowledge in the world. He created the vast library of tablets that was discovered in the excavation of Nineveh and would later be known as the Royal Library of Ashurbanipal. His passion for education and literature led to the preservation of the ways and knowledge of the time, and we have him to thank for protecting many of the stories recorded in this book! The tablets at Nineveh outnumbered any other collection and were in the best condition when they were recovered.

Ashurbanipal was the last of the great Assyrian kings. After he died, a civil war ensued as three different men vied for the crown. The division of forces left the Assyrians ripe for conquest, and the marauding nomadic tribes of the east, the Scythians and Cimmerians, looted and pillaged a wide swath through the Assyrian Empire. Over the coming centuries, the Mesopotamian region plunged into constant civil war, resulting in widespread devastation. By 500 BCE, there was nothing beyond empty cities, dried-up fields, and a complete scattering of the once great civilizations that thrived there. Alexander the Great swept through the area many years later and attempted to revitalize it. He was marginally successful, but it was not until the Romans came that order was truly restored. However, the culture of Mesopotamia had been altered forever. The gods were lost and their mythology forgotten. Under the later conquest of the Islamic state, the history and lore of Mesopotamia were further buried until, thanks to archeological digs that began in the 1800s, it was rediscovered.

# Chapter 2 Creation Myths

Most civilizations have creation myths that tell the story of how man came to be on the Earth. The ancient Mesopotamians had three main versions that share some similarities while having their own unique twist on the central themes. Let us begin with the earliest people, the Sumerians, and therefore, the earliest creation myth, the Eridu Genesis. Of course, being the oldest means the written record has sustained more damage over time. However, piecing together several different tablets, hymns, and poems from that era gives us a pretty good idea of the Sumerian theory of creation. It is important to note that while told in a single-story form here, this is a compilation of texts that came from several different sources.

## The Eridu Genesis

Before the dawn of time, Nammu, the goddess of creation, brought forth the universe known as Anki and the primordial waters known as Abuz. Anki called forth from the wind the god Enlil. From the Abuz, Anki created the heavens and the god Anu. Anu created the Earth and its goddess, Ki. There was a time of darkness where heaven and earth were joined. There was no light, but the earth thrived with living green plants. The Abuz, the water of life, flowed beneath the ground giving life to all things. Enlil, master of the air and wind, separated the heavens from the earth and gave Anu and Ki control over their domains.

Enlil and Ki had a child, Enki, to whom was given the Earth and sea to control. Enki sought to improve the Earth and went to Nammu for blessed water to create rivers. With the water from Nammu, he created the Euphrates and the Tigris and brought life to the region. He improved the soil, made plants grow, and animals thrive.

Other gods and goddesses were brought forth at this time as well. Temples were created, and in their respective temples, the gods and goddesses

9

dwelled, waited on by lesser deities. Ninlil, the goddess of grain, was exceedingly beautiful. Ninlil had been warned not to bathe in the river where Enlil could see her, for he would want to lie with her if he saw her beauty. Ninlil did not heed the advice and went to bathe in the river. Enlil attempted to seduce her, but she rebuffed him. He refused to be denied and took her by force. Ninlil ended up pregnant, and Enlil was banished for his behavior.

Ninlil, though she had refused him, did not want Enlil to miss out on the birth of their child. She followed him throughout his banishment. Her child was to be the god of the moon, but the rulers of the Underworld demanded restitution for the one who would never dwell there. So, as Ninlil followed behind Enlil throughout his wanderings, he seduced her on three separate occasions. She bore three other children who were given to the Underworld and dwelt there as gods. As for her first child, Sin, he went to dwell in the sky as the moon with supreme powers of divination and prophecy.

Now that the heavens and earth were formed, the gods lived in their glory for many millennia. Eventually, the lesser gods became weary of being the servants of the higher gods. They did not like being the only ones who worked at digging ditches, tending animals, or building temples. They rebelled against the higher gods and rioted outside of Enlil's temple.

Enlil did not know what to do with the angry mob, so he sought out Enki and Anu. Together, they decided that they needed to create a kind of being who would do all the things the lesser gods were complaining about. Geshtu-e was a god of great cunning and wisdom. He was picked to be sacrificed so from his blood they could create their new race of beings. The Mother Goddess, Ninmah, used her powers of creation to mix Geshtu-e's blood into clay.

Ninmah and Enki took the clay into the sacred room of the temple and worked magic into the clay. Ninmah took the clay and broke it into fourteen pieces and placed them in her womb. She carried them, seven men, and seven women until she gave birth to the first humans.

The gods were much pleased with their handiwork, and there was a great celebration following the birth of the humans. During the festivities, Enki and Ninmah began to bicker about their role in forming the humans. Ninmah felt she was responsible for how well a human was formed, and the form was of paramount importance. However, Enki said that did not matter since regardless of their physical form, he could help them thrive in society. Ninmah described humans with a myriad of afflictions challenging Enki to create a suitable use for the less than perfect human. She could not best him as he placed even the most afflicted person in a suitable occupation. Enki then challenged Ninmah to do the same. He created a truly wretched creature who was twisted and malformed, and Ninmah could not think of anything the wretch would be good for. She also recognized that if she let many humans be born with such deformities, they would not have faith or be loyal to her. Ninmah was frustrated and angry. Enki decided that he wanted to make peace with her. He said that while he did have the power to create people, they would not be complete without her divine influence. They set aside their argument and agreed to make new life together, so it could be as perfect as they could make it.

After the creation of man, the gods then enjoyed the creatures they had made. They enjoyed having humans as their servants and the progression of the humans as a race. The humans erected cities, including Eridu, and the first kings were appointed by the gods. As mankind began to flourish, the gods soon realized that they were harder to govern than they thought they would be. The humans started to expand and build more and more cities and infrastructure. They dug canals and built walls. It all created a lot of havoc and noise. This displeased some of the gods, especially Enlil. He decided that they should destroy mankind.

The other gods did not like this plan, but none of them were willing to oppose Enlil. King Ziusudra was a powerful king and a favorite among the gods. He worshipped daily at the statue of the god Enki. When he stood at the statue one day, he witnessed a vision. In the vision, the gods discussed the fate of mankind, deciding that they should be eradicated, and took an oath not to reveal their plan to anyone.

While Ziusudra stood gaping at the statue trying to understand what he had just seen, the voice of Enki, the god of the sea, came from the wall. It whispered of the plans to flood the region and wipe out humanity. Enki told Ziusudra to build a large boat and to carry onto it animals, plants, and precious things.

Ziusudra did as he was told and just as he finished the boat, the storms came. The rains raged for seven days and seven nights, and all of the land was swallowed in an ocean. Once the storm was over, Ziusudra made offerings to the gods. Enlil was very angry that he had been disobeyed, but Enki stood by his actions. In the end, Enlil granted Ziusudra immortality but banished him to live outside the realm of man.

This was the first version of the flood myth that describes the devastation and revitalization of mankind in the Mesopotamian region. It is played out in several different cultures and appears later in great detail in the Epic of Gilgamesh. On top of the Eridu Genesis, there are several short disputations that illuminate how certain aspects of the world established themselves. These debates give further insight into how these early people view the world and the balance within it.

# <u>The Sumerian Disputations</u>
## The Debate Between Grain and Sheep

These short poems each stand alone, but they do discuss the early days of the gods and man. In the Debate Between the Grain and Sheep, the world was still new. People roamed it naked and ignorant. They ate grass like sheep and drank from ditches. The gods created grain and sheep, and they partook of both. It pleased them, and they sent the grain and sheep down from their sacred mountain to mankind. Mankind planted the grain and raised the sheep, and they brought prosperity to the region. Lahar, the goddess of cattle and beasts, and Ashar, the goddess of grain, saw that both sheep and grain thrived. They fell into a rivalry and began to debate who was more important.

Lahar claimed, "I feed and clothe the workers and am strong of body! Ashar, your body is pounded into flour!"

Ashar retaliated, "Your sheep must be kept in pens and scatter to wind at the least sound or scare! I feed your animals and make them strong. They would be nothing without me!"

And so, the two goddesses fought and argued until Enki intervened. He spoke to Enlil, and Enlil spoke the judgment, "You are sisters, but grain is superior. Lahar, fall to your knees and kiss her feet!"

## The Debate Between Winter and Summer

Another disputation that gives insight into the shaping of the world is the Debate Between Winter and Summer. Enlil set his mind to improving the Earth. He wanted to see it flourish and bloom with prosperity. He set one foot on the earth like a bull stomping a mighty hoof and decided the Earth should have two seasons, winter and summer. To bring them into the world, Enlil copulated with a hill and planted into the womb of the Earth the two seasons. When night fell, the hill opened her womb to release the seasons.

Enlil nurtured them in pastures of the mountains while he designed their destinies. To Summer, he gave sunlight, growth, and abundance. It was a time to build and to create. To Winter, he gave the blessed rain from which all life would spring. He made it a time of plenty and rest where the toils of the summer bore fruit.

Winter and Summer both matured and turned their hands to their tasks. Winter filled the Tigris and Euphrates and made ponds, lakes, and lagoons. He filled the rivers with fishes and water birds. Summer made the land fertile for planting and created towns, houses, and temples. He made the plants grow, and the animals thrive.

Of course, as brothers often do, they began to argue about who was better than the other. They took their argument to Enlil. Enlil answered decisively, "Winter controls water which brings life to all things. Summer, how could you be equal to this?" That settled the argument, for Enlil's judgment was never questioned. The brothers had a huge celebration, and Summer presented Winter with offerings of lapis-lazuli and precious metals. From then on, Summer and Winter were in perfect harmony, and the Earth knew balance and symmetry.

## The Debate Between Bird and Fish

In the Debate Between Bird and Fish, Enki is the featured god, and the first part of the poem offers a glimpse into the role he played in shaping the world. Enki, master of creation, set about filling the world with life in the early days of the Earth. He filled the sheep and cattle pens with animals. He caused the Euphrates and Tigris to flow swiftly. He made the black-haired people reproduce and grow in numbers. He stocked the waters with fish and the sky with birds. Enki also established the first kings to guide the people and made them sovereign among the humans.

In the animal world, the bird and the fish both sought to live in the lakes and streams. The fish complained to the bird that it was making too much noise in the lakes and was too greedy, eating fish, spawn, and plants. The fish said that the bird was nothing but a nuisance who had to be kept from ruining the fields and was only good for being fattened up to be served on a plate.

The bird, of course, took great offense to this and retorted, "You're one to talk! You, with your round mouth, you do not even have a neck to turn and look around. You stink, and the people cannot even stand to touch you!" Thus, began a bitter rivalry between the bird and the fish.

The fish could not abide sharing the water with the bird, so he swam silently through the depths of the waters and destroyed the bird's nest from beneath. The eggs spilled out and broke. The bird screeched with indignation and ruthlessly destroyed the fish's spawn by pulling them from the water and eating them. They raged at each other until the fish said that they should seek out wise Enki to settle the matter.

Together they took their grievances to Enki, who was not happy with their bickering and fighting. He told them about the order of things in nature and judged the bird to be higher in that order than the fish. The bird had a sweet song and delicious meat that was fit for the table of the gods. The bird also could travel both on land in the water, making him superior to the fish. The fish accepted the verdict and his place in the order of the world.

# Enki and the World Order

This myth picks up the same tack as the Sumerian Disputations. It seeks to shape the world after it was created. In a world that was brand new, there must have been a lot to sort out and Enki, wisest and cleverest of the lot, was just the god for the job. The poem opens with a long hymn singing Enki's praises, saying that he could assess a situation with a glance and know exactly what is needed to be done. Enlil has given a job to do—set the world in order. No small job, but one that Enki feels completely capable of doing!

This was an important job, and Enki did not take it lightly. He recognized how important it was to organize the chaos and make everything in the universe fit together. His plan included everything from the grass in the meadows to the duties and roles of the gods. He covered the Earth, spreading abundance and virility.

Enki brought forth many different animals as he surveyed the barren plains. He created bison, wild sheep, and stag. He rooted the mountains deep into the Earth. He made the meadows green and encouraged water to flow freely from the Apsu. He also organized the days and nights and instructed the priests on different rights and rituals to observe.

Once he had done all of this and much more, Enki stood back to observe his handiwork. He gets into his boat and begins to make his way through the marshes to the different cities he has created. Nimgirsig, the captain of his boat, steers them through the large expanse of marshlands and Enki thought about how much he loved this wet and wild place. It was truly his element.

They stopped first at Eridu, home of Enki's temple and the seat of his cult power. The people had prepared the city for his arrival. The priests had cleansed and purified the temple. They had built a beautiful staircase down to the new quayside that was the launch into the Apsu. They pulled into the quayside, and Enki stepped onto land, looking over his city. He raised his hands and blessed the city in the name of Enlil. He finished his blessing with,

"May your cattle be numerous. May your sheep pens be many and overflowing with sheep. May your temples kiss the heavens!"

Then Enki got back in the boat and went to inspect the city, Ur. He looked out over the city and sealed its destiny. "Great city of Ur, you are well-established and prosperous. You are favored by Enlil and are pleasing to the gods. Your shrine shall rise to heaven!"

Next, Nimgirsig steered the boat to Kur Meluhha. There he looked up at the huge looming black trees and thick reed beds that clogged the marshes. It was a fertile and strong city, and Enki was pleased. He blessed it like he had Ur but spoke specifically of some of its natural resources. "Your black trees are mighty and noble. Let them make the thrones of kings. Your reeds are strong and true. Let them be our weapons on the battlefield. Your bulls will be large and know no rival! Your gold will be silver, and your copper will be bronze-tin. You will be fruitful and blessed!"

On to Dilmun, they traveled. The land was impure and overrun with enemies of the Sumerians. Enki frowned as he watched them eat the dates and pull fish after fish from the lagoons. He cleansed the land, vanquishing the invading Elamites, and claiming all of their treasures as an offering for Enlil.

On his travels, Enki encounters a nomadic tribe of the Martu. He blesses them with cattle, and they were allowed to continue their roaming. Enki brought abundant grain to the river valley and saw that Enlil's storehouse in Nippur was stuffed full. He felt like he was starting to get a handle on how the world was shaping up.

Once he was done inspecting the world, he was full of energy and purpose. He saw something else that needed to be tended to. He filled the Euphrates and Tigris rivers with his semen so they "gave birth" to water and life to the river. This was also probably the origin of the Sumerian custom for a male to ejaculate into the rivers to add virility and life into the waters that provided them with the very essence of life. Enki left Enbilulu, the god of canals and waterways, in charge of the mighty rivers.

Enki then filled the marshlands with fish and reinforced the reed beds. He assigned an unknown god to watch over these important resources. Then, he realized that the gods needed a place to congregate and he created a magnificent temple within the marsh. It was a grand palace with an interior that was more intricate than any maze. The gods beheld the gift and were pleased. They sang praises to Enki and held a great celebration.

Enki entrusted the care of the temple to the Lady of the Storerooms, the goddess Nanse. Nanse held the powers of fresh water, fertility, and justice – in particular, social justice. Her talents with ensuring bounty and balance made her an ideal candidate for the task.

Now that the palace of the gods was situated, Enki created the rains. He gathered clouds in the sky and filled them with life-giving rain. These he gave to the god Adad, a storm god who could wield both lightning and thunder. His storm chariot would pull the clouds across the heavens and ensure the livelihood of the people on Earth.

Organizing agriculture was next on Enki's list. He summoned the plow and yokes and created teams of oxen to pull them. He plowed furrows in the ground and planted fields. He called Enkimdu, Enlil's farmer and keeper of ditches and dikes, to be Master of the Fields. Enki blessed Enkimdu with the wisdom of planting, harvesting, and tending crops.

Enki blessed the newly planted crops, and they flourished. They stuffed the storehouses full of grain. Ashar, goddess of grain, was given charge of making sure the grain flowed from the fields and kept the storerooms filled. She was also tasked with teaching people how to bake bread, the food of all.

To the god Kulla, Enki gave the responsibility of tending the temples and keeping them in good repair. As the god of bricks, Kulla's buildings were straight and true. His foundations were strong, and he brought with him blessings to any building he created.

Enki moved on to the plains again and let his abundance wash over all the animals of the plains. With his divine wisdom, he swelled their numbers to their peak, without losing the balance of nature. He called the shepherd Dumuzid to his side and charged him with maintaining that balance.

Throughout the lands, Enki established temples. He wanted the gods to have a place to rest and work on the Earth. Opulent and grand, the temples pleased the gods, and there was more celebration.

Finally, Enki was almost finished with his organization. The last two gods he summoned were Shamash and Uttu. To Shamash, he gave the weighty responsibility of the entire universe. He was to maintain balance with his powers of justice and fate. Turning to Uttu, he gave his last instructions after he created the loom. Uttu, the spider goddess, was tasked with teaching women how to weave cloth.

Enki was finished. He was most pleased with his work. As he sought to retire, Ishtar confronted him. "You have given jobs and responsibilities to everyone except me," she cried. "I am the Queen of Heaven, the mighty Ishtar! You gave each of my sisters something to do. Ninmah is the midwife to the Earth and watches over new life. Ninsun stands next to Anu, speaking as she likes to him. The Wild Cow of the Heavens, she has been blessed! My other sister, Ninmug, has taken up a chisel of gold. She makes the crowns of kings. Ninsaba has her reeds and measuring tape. The scholars worship her, and the scribe bow to her. Of course, Nanse is out judging fishes with her precious pelican and making sure everything is in balance. And what of me? Will I get the blessing like my sisters? Nay! You did not give anything to me! It simply isn't fair!"

Enki, well acquainted with Ishtar's temper and theatrics, listened as she implacably ranted. He, perfect in wisdom and foresight, had not simply forgotten about Ishtar. He also knew that what he was about to say would not make her happy, but it had to be said nonetheless.

"My Lady Ishtar, Queen of the Heavens, Goddess of Love, Beauty and War, how have you been wronged? Are you not the most beautiful of the gods? Do you not have bright robes of the best cloth? Does your hair not shine brighter than any jewel? Is your voice not sweeter than any honey? Do you not have through your husband, the god of the shepherds, Dumuzid, the staff of the shepherd under your control?" He paused to let some of this sink in and then continued, "Ishtar, you command chariots of war and destruction. You can bring order to chaos or weave disorder into tranquility. Your might and power are already unparalleled!"

Ishtar had to admit he had a point. She preened like a peacock under Enki's praise, but he was not yet done with his lecture.

"Yes, you are indeed a goddess of much power and ability. You already have more than what all of your sisters have, but what do you do with it? You leave piles of heads in your wake without a thought. At a whim, you lock away the instruments that raise sweet music and silence the hymns and lamentations. Your vanity and idleness are legendary. You have not used your gifts to improve my world, and that, my Lady Queen of Heaven, is why you were not trusted with anything more."

Ishtar's rage swelled at the rebuff, but Enki cut her off before she could retort. "The Mighty Enlil and Father Anu are pleased with the world order, and it will be as I said. Now go from me and think on my counsel."

And thus, the order and balance were brought to the world. Oh, praise be to Enki, mighty creator, and father of man!

# Enuma Elis

Another version of the flood myth is the Babylonian version called the Enuma Elis. This myth dates to around the 12th century BCE. Enlil was replaced as the head of the pantheon by Marduk, though he and Anu still remained very high in the ranks and well respected. Marduk's rise parallels the rise of Babylon as a preeminent city in the region. Several versions of the poem exist, but the most intact version was discovered in the great library of Nineveh. It contains just over 1,000 lines and spans four clay tablets. It was often used as practice for scribes to hone their handwriting skills and translations in both Akkadian and Assyrian dialects have been found.

*Note: The God Enki, god of the sea, is known as Ea at this point in Sumerian mythology.*

Before there was anything, before the sky or earth, before man or god, there were two entities: Tiamat and Apsu. They dwelt on a different plane than that of today's mortal men for there was no earth or heavens at that time. Tiamat was the ocean, vast and deep, and Apsu was clear, fresh water. When they came together as husband and wife, the first pair of gods was created. Lahmu and Lahamu were brought forth from the primordial waters of Tiamat and Apsu. Lahmu and Lahamu were the stars and the zodiac, and the universe was contained within them.

Lahmu and Lahamu brought forth Anshar and Kishar, who contained the heavens and the earth, respectively. Finally, Anshar created Anu, the god of the heavens and father supreme of the gods, and Anu created Ea, the god of water, creation, and knowledge. These new gods were unsettled and created chaos in the previously still world of Apsu and Tiamat. Apsu, unable to settle the fledgling gods, was displeased at being disturbed and called his advisor, Mummu to him. Together, Apsu and Mummu spoke to Tiamat about the disruption, and Mummu counseled his masters to destroy the newly formed gods. Tiamat was reluctant and pleaded with Apsu to be patient. However, Apsu was firm in his decision.

The gods heard of the plan to eradicate them, and they came together in a council. They looked to Ea, the god of knowledge, for a plan to save them. Ea crafted a spell and cast it upon Apsu, sending him into a deep slumber. Mummu tried to wake his master, but he could not. Ea took it a step further and killed Apsu, taking his crown for himself. He bound Mummu and cast him away. Ea and his wife, Damkina, took over Apsu's realm, and they had a child, Marduk.

Marduk surpassed all the other gods in physical prowess and magical power. Anu created the wind and gave it to Marduk to control. He urged Marduk to set the winds free to punish Tiamat. Marduk gave the winds free rein. They gusted and surged, creating havoc and once again, disrupting the peace.

Tiamat was upset by the winds, but she was not the only one. Many of the other gods complained to her and asked her to stand up to Marduk. She consented to help and created an army of monsters. They were terrible beasts – scorpion-men, serpents, bull-men, and dragons. They had vicious fangs, and poison ran through their veins. Besides her army of monsters, she created eleven terrible warriors, who were even more monstrous than the others. They were enormous and were armed with fierce weapons. Lastly, she promoted Qingu to war chief and took him as her consort. She bestowed upon him the Tablets of Destiny and imbued him with the same level of power as Anu. Thus, whatever Qingu decreed would come to be, and he was suddenly equal to the mightiest of gods.

When Ea saw the army Tiamat had amassed, he became very concerned. He went to his father, Ashar for advice. Ashar was greatly troubled by what was happening among the gods. He advised Ea to try to talk to Tiamat and soothe her ire. Ea left his father and sought out Tiamat. However, his courage failed him as he beheld her monstrous preparations. He returned to his father without attempting to speak to her. Ea asked his father to send someone else. Anu attempted to lay a spell to quiet Tiamat, but he, too, was unsuccessful.

Ashar spoke to the Assembly of Gods and asked for a volunteer to face Tiamat. Ea prompted his son, Marduk, to take up the call to arms. Marduk, who was as full of confidence and arrogance as a god could be, happily volunteered. Marduk told his grandfather, Ashar, that he would present Tiamat at Ashar's feet. Ashar gave him his blessing and urged him to go forth and join in battle with the fearsome goddess. Before Marduk was willing to go into battle, he told his grandfather, "Since I am saving your lives, I will have a reward! I will reign supreme among the gods. My word will never be changed or challenged and what I create shall never be undone!"

Marduk called his advisor, Kakka, and dispatched him to convene all of the great gods, including Lahmu, Lahamu, Kishar, and Anshar. At Marduk's command, all of the gods who were not supporting Tiamat were called together, and Kakka explained what Tiamat had been up to and no one, not even Ea or Anu, had been able to confront her. Many of the great gods were unaware of Tiamat's activities as they were much removed from that realm. However, upon hearing of the uprising, they were disturbed. While they discussed what was to be done, wine, ale, and food flowed freely. When they were drowsy and probably more than a little tipsy, Kakka pressed the point that Marduk was willing to take on Tiamat in exchange for supremacy among the gods. In their befuddled state, the gods could not come up with any other plan and agreed to support Marduk and his demands.

The gods set up a shrine to Marduk and paid him homage. They presented him with offerings and weapons to go forth and defeat Tiamat. He took up his bow and arrow and his mace. He filled his body with fire and created a net of lightning to ensnare Tiamat. Marduk harnessed his storm chariot and to it the fearsome team of four – Slayer, Racer, Pitiless, and Flyer. Their teeth were coated with poison, and they would never tire in battle. Marduk also called the winds. He stirred the four winds and cast them into Tiamat. Then, he added seven more winds, a tempest, a cyclone, and the unfaceable wind. He drove his chariot behind the swath of chaos created by his winds.

Marduk drove to the center of Tiamat, seeking Qingu so he could discover his adversary's plans. Tiamat spoke sweetly to him, "See how big your army is! See how mighty you are, Marduk, King of Gods! All of the gods sit in your palace, oh Mighty One!"

Marduk answered, "You are not fooling me with your sweet words! I know all about your army of monsters. I know that you plan to kill your children! Where is your compassion? Where is your tolerance? How could you usurp the powers of Anu and give them to your lover, Qingu? You are treacherous and wicked! Let your army ready themselves. I will conquer them after I have defeated you!"

Tiamat was incensed by this, and she launched herself at Marduk. She summoned her magic as she and Marduk locked in single combat. Marduk encircled her in his net of lightning, and when she opened her mouth to speak her spell, Marduk choked her with the evil wind. She swallowed the wind, and it expanded inside her, threatening to make her explode. Marduk shot his arrow through Tiamat's gut and split her in half, killing her.

The gods who had supported Tiamat cowered and shook in fear of retribution. Marduk spared their lives but took their weapons and cast them into the same net with Tiamat's remains. He gathered her monsters and bound them. Marduk fought and subdued Qingu, who he saw as unworthy to wield the power he was given. He took the Tablets of Destiny and kept them for himself. Once the battlefield was secure, Marduk split open Tiamat's head and spilled her blood on the North Wind. It was carried back to the Assembly of Gods, letting them know of Marduk's victory. They celebrated and readied gifts to give the conquering hero upon his return.

Marduk considered Tiamat's corpse. With it, he created many marvelous creations before he separated her in half. He stretched one half over the heavens and created the sky. The other half, he spread below it and created the Earth, crafting mountains and valleys. With the vapors of Tiamat, the clouds, fog, and weather were made. Using the water from her eyes, Marduk filled the Euphrates and Tigris rivers. In the heavens, he arranged the stars in patterns and set the moon to a monthly schedule, designing a twelve-month year. In the heavens, he created palaces for Enlil, Ea, and Anu. Finally, happy with his work, Marduk returned to join the celebration with his fellow gods.

Marduk was received like the champion he was. The other gods bowed and kissed his feet. They rained down presents and blessings upon their new king. Marduk accepted their offerings and their allegiance. Then, he announced that he would build a shrine for himself upon the Earth. It would be a grand and sacred place, fit for the king he was. Marduk proclaimed that all the gods would be welcome there, and it would be a respite for them. He said he would name it Babylon.

Marduk decided, as the king of gods, he needed to do something about the toils of the lesser gods. They complained bitterly about being servants to the higher gods. He counseled with his father, Ea. He told Ea, "I will make a race from blood and bone. They shall be known as men. They will serve us, and we will be at our leisure."

Ea suggested that they sacrifice a god who was among the traitors that followed Tiamat. Marduk called the gods together and demanded whoever started the war and roused Tiamat to violence should be brought forward. The gods quickly identified Qingu. Without any further deliberation, Ea cut off his head to use his blood to make mankind.

Once mankind was created, and the gods were free of their labors, Marduk divided them. He sent 300 of the host of gods to dwell in the heavens, and 600 were to dwell on Earth. The gods were much pleased with their new king and in their exuberance, they offered to build his shrine. Marduk commanded them to build Babylon. For the next year, they fashioned bricks. The following year, they constructed the great temple, Esagila, the sacred temple of Marduk.

Upon completion of the temple, Marduk hosted a huge banquet. All of the gods gathered and paid homage to him. All of his fifty names were read and praised individually. In closing, the gods were admonished to remember the great deeds of Marduk and the importance of having a good, strong king to lead them.

# Atrahasis

There is one more major creation myth in Mesopotamian lore. It includes the familiar flood myth as well as the creation of mankind to alleviate the burden of work from the gods. It is believed to have been written initially in Akkadian, but fragments of tablets with the tale translated into Assyrian have also been recovered. It is thought to have originated around 1625 BCE. The creation theme in Atrahasis is the creation of man, not the gods or the world.

There was once a time, before the creation of man, when the gods toiled making the Earth. The seven great gods of the Anunnaki lorded over the Igigi, the lesser deities. The Igigi were forced to work the land while the Anunnaki supervised. They moved the earth to create the mighty Euphrates River followed by the Tigris River. Then, the Igigi raised the mountains and tapped into the primordial waters of Apsu to fill the rivers and canals they dug. For over forty years, they toiled under the instruction of the Anunnaki.

The Igigi grew tired of their work and enslavement. They complained bitterly and finally rose up in rebellion. They focused their ire on Enlil, the perfect foreman, who had ordered them around for all those years. In defiance, they burned their tools and workbaskets and set fire to the construction sites. They marched on Enlil's temple, Ekur, and surrounded it.

It was the middle of the night, and Enlil was unaware that he was under attack. His doorkeeper, Kalkal, was on duty and barred the door from the invaders. He called to Nuska, Enlil's chief advisor, and bade him go and awake their master. Nuska woke Enlil and told him of the threat at his gates.

Enlil called for his weapons and said to Nuska, "Arm yourself and stand in front of me!"

Nuska looked at his master and was shocked to see the fear on his face. "My Lord! Why are you afraid of your own sons? Call to the Mighty Father Anu and wise Enki. Have them come here and seek their support."

Acting on the wise words of his counselor, he called to Anu and Enki and the other great gods. Once the Anunnaki was assembled in his court, he asked them, "Do you see the rabble at my gate? What am I to do here? Why are they rising against me?"

Anu advised, "Send Nuska out to them and let him hear their grievances."

Enlil spoke to Nuska, saying, "Go to the Igigi and bow to them. Ask them, in the name of their father Anu, these questions: Who is in charge? Who leads the fighting? Who led them to my door? Who has declared war on me?"

Nuska wasted no time. He took up his weapons and went out to take his master's message to the Igigi. The Igigi listened to the questions and answered him as one, "Every one of us has declared war on Enlil! We work and work! It is too much! Every one of us marched on his door, and every one of us will fight!"

Nuska dutifully returned to the Anunnaki with the Igigi's response. Enlil was saddened and angered by the response. He turned to Anu and said, "O Father of All, show them your power! Sacrifice one of their numbers as an example of what happens when they rebel against us!"

Enki intervened and spoke firmly, "Did we not hear the warnings? Have we not ignored their complaints and grumbling? Their work is too much, and their despair is too great! We cannot punish them for something we have ignored!" The other gods were uncertain of what to do so Enki proposed a solution. "Nintu, goddess of the womb, you can create another race, a race of man. Man can take up the yoke of the burden from the Igigi. They will do their duties, so the Igigi can know leisure and rest!"

Nintu shook her head. "Enki, you are the god of creation. I cannot make them without your help. Enki, you must give me the clay, and then I can make the race of man."

Enki agreed, saying, "I will perform a purification ritual on the first, seventh, and fifteenth day. Then you shall have your clay. We will sacrifice Ilwela, who has extreme intelligence and use his blood to mix with the clay. Ilwela's spirit shall not be forgotten but will live as a ghost to his memory!"

The Anunnaki were in agreement, and the plan was carried out.

Nintu used the flesh and blood of Ilwela to mix with clay, and all of the gods of the Anunnaki and Igigi spat upon the mixed clay. Nintu stood in front of the assembly and said, "I have done my job, and soon the race of man will take up the yoke of the burden from the Igigi. You have given over your troubles and noise to mankind. Hear me, Igigi, you are free!"

The Igigi rejoiced at her words, and they fell down to worship her. They cried out, "Thank you, Blessed Mami! From now on you will be known as Mother of all Gods!"

Nintu and Enki went into the sacred room of fates and began the process of turning clay into man. Enki worked the clay while Nintu spoke spells and incantations over it. Then, Nintu took the clay and broke it into fourteen pieces. She divided the pieces into groups of seven and separated them by a mud brick.

The womb goddesses were called forth and helped Nintu create a womb for the clay pieces. Nintu set down rules that day for the governance of childbirth. She said, "When a woman is giving birth, a mud brick should be put down for seven days. The wise Mami shall be honored in the house. When the babe is born, the midwife shall celebrate, and the mother shall cut herself free from the babe. Men and women shall come together when a woman comes into her bosom, and a man has hair on his face. They shall choose each other and be happy!"

28

With those decrees, the womb incubated for ten months. Nintu then broke open the womb, and the first man was born. She rejoiced as the midwife and cut cords as the mother, thus setting the expectation of accordance to her rules.

The human race was born, and they flourished. Men and women divided the tasks between them and the gods' burdens were lifted. For almost 1200 years, the human race grew and expanded. They built cities, dug canals, established fields of grain and herds of animals, and sustained the gods. They were also noisy and dirty, and all of their movements and activities unsettled and disturbed the gods.

Enlil, in particular, had reached his breaking point. He decided to send a plague to decrease the population.

As the illness gripped the region, Atrahasis prayed to his god, Enki. "Why are the gods angry with us? For how long must we suffer?"

Enki answered his faithful servant, "Spread the word among the people. Call together the elders and let the heralds call it from on high. Do not pray to your patron gods! Lift your voices and send your offerings to Namtara! Ask him to lift the scourge in the land. Offer him a baked loaf and your devotion. He will be shamed into lifting the curse!"

Atrahasis did as he was told. The people built a temple for Namtara and brought him loaves upon loaves of bread. They prayed and showered Namtara with devotion. As Enki predicted, Namtara could not sustain a plague among people who showed him such love and affection. The plague was wiped from the land.

Another 1200 years passed and again the humans became too noisy and bothersome for the gods' sensibilities. The humans were interrupting the gods' rest and peace. Enlil ordered his fellow gods, "We will send a famine. Adad dry up your rain and let not a drop fall from the sky. The earth shall go fallow, and no crops shall grow. Nissaba, withdraw your bounty. Stop the flow of the rivers, and let the winds roll across the lands until they are stripped bare!"

The gods followed Enlil's instructions. Again, the exceedingly wise Atrahasis was counseled by his god, Enki. Enki whispered to Atrahasis in response to his prayers, "Tell your people! Let the heralds shout from the rooftops. Forsake your patron gods. Raise your voices to Mighty Adad. Lay your offerings at his feet. Shower him with your prayers. He will bring the mists and then a drop of dew. In the night, he will ride his chariot across the sky pulling the rain behind him. Your harvest will be nine-fold!"

Atrahasis heard Enki's words and hastened to tell everyone. The heralds shouted the message, and Adad was soon the center of worship. Temples were built, and offerings were made. Soon, Adad could not ignore his faithful people's plight. Like a thief in the night, he brought the rains, and the drought was ended.

A third era of relative peace passed, but eventually, mankind once again became too much for the gods to bear. This time Enlil issued his harshest orders. "Anu and Adad, you will lock the heavens away from the earth. No rain or sun shall escape. Nergal and Sin shall blight the earth and dry up her womb, so she produces nothing. Enki you shall stop up the flow of the rivers and canals."

The gods followed their instructions, and the earth became barren. The people ate through their stores over the next two years. By the third year, there was widespread starvation. The people grew sick and stooped with malnutrition. By the sixth year, families began to turn on each other, and there were disturbing rumors of cannibalism.

Atrahasis prayed and prayed to his god, Enki. He sent him offerings and slept by the dried-up river bed so he could hear his instructions.

Enki could not bear the suffering of the humans any longer. He unlocked the waters of the rivers and let them flow forth full of fish to feed the remaining people. Enlil was furious, and he called together the Assembly of the Gods.

Enki and the other gods listened as Enlil raged on and on about his attempts to eradicate the humans and how they were all foiled by Enki. Enki did not accept Enlil's judgment and argued, "These are people of our creation! They have the blood of a god in their veins and were created to lighten our loads! How can you send such suffering to your own people?"

Enlil was not to be swayed, and he ignored Enki's words. "You, Enki, will send a flood, and we will be rid of the humans for good. We are all in agreement, and it will be so!" The gods were not all in agreement, but none of them had the guts to stand up to Enlil in his rage – except Enki.

Enki shook his head, furious with Enlil and the other gods. "How can you ask this of me? How can you ask me to kill all of my people? I cannot even conceive of it! This is your dirty work, Enlil! You do it! I will not!"

It was a valiant effort by Enki to save his people, but in the end, it was not enough. The other gods supported Enlil's verdict. Enki was forced to take an oath that he would not help the people and that he would send a flood to wipe the earth clean of mankind.

Enki could not break his oath and warn the people. However, he was not the wisest of all the gods for nothing. He whispered his instructions to the wall of Atrahasis' house. That night as Atrahasis slept, he heard the words in a vision. Since Enki had not directly told Atrahasis, he did not technically break his oath.

In his dream, Atrahasis was told to leave his house and build a boat. He was told not to worry about material wealth and only take with him living things. The boat must be built exceedingly strong and should have a roof. The whole boat should be able to be sealed as if it was meant to go to the depths of the sea. Atrahasis saw an hourglass that held seven days of sand and knew that the storm would rage for seven days and seven nights. When Atrahasis woke, he knew what needed to be done.

The Elders of the city waited for him as he emerged from his sleep. He said to them, "My god, Enki, is out of favor with your god, Enlil. They are very angry with each other, and Enlil has decreed that I cannot stay here. I am to go down into the Apsu and dwell with Enki there."

The city pitched together and helped Atrahasis build his boat. He brought on board his family and all the animals he could find. He hosted a feast for the village but could not enjoy it, knowing what was to come. The weather suddenly changed, and Adad led the storms across the sky.

Thunder crashed, and the winds roared as Atrahasis closed up the boat and cut it free. The storm raged and raged. The people of the Earth could not stand before it. They were like defenseless sheep and were swept away in the raging tide.

Nintu watched in horror, and she began to weep. She cried, "How could I have condoned this? How could I have not stood against Enlil and Anu? They did not take counsel, but set their minds on this horrific deed! How could a creator turn destroyer? How am I to live? I shall stay forever in the house of mourning!"

Nintu's wails and distress were felt by many of the other gods. They joined her in her lament. For seven days and seven nights, the storm raged, and the gods watched what they had wrought. They longed for beer and sustenance, but there was no one there to get it for them. They yearned for offerings, but there was no one left to make them. Great was their regret and despair.

When the storm abated, to their great surprise, they smelled the offering of food. The gods flocked to the smell like flies to a carcass. They devoured the offering, and Nintu once again launched into blaming Anu and Enlil. "How dare you come to this offering? You care not for the creature who left it! I will never forget again how blessed the people of our creation are!"

Enlil, of course, was angry when he discovered that Atrahasis had survived the flood. "How did this happen? All were meant to perish! We all took an oath!"

Anu spoke up, "Who else but Enki could have made this happen? He made sure the reed house sent the vision to Atrahasis."

Enki stood tall and proud. "I defied you and your oath! I ensured that life was preserved! You can punish me if you must, but I did what I knew was right!"

Enlil told Enki, "If you and Nintu love the humans so much, devise a way that they will not grow so noisy in the future."

Enki and Nintu sat in conference and decreed that people would now die. Nintu and Enki would also ensure that a third of pregnancies would not succeed. They created a she-demon who would snatch babes from their mother and take them to the Underworld. Finally, they created priestesses who would have to remain celibate. All of these measures were put in place to keep the population in check so there would never be a need for another great flood.

Interestingly, Atrahasis appears to have been an actual king. His name is on the Sumerian List of Kings in the pre-flood group. He was the king of Shuruppak, where the patron god was Ninlil, goddess of grain.

The creation myths give insight into the basic belief system of the ancient Mesopotamians, namely the gods created man to serve them. They also establish the gods as vengeful and sometimes petty. There are theories that when a particular version of a myth is slanted for or against a specific god, it is because the scribes that copied that text were priests in that god's temple. For example, the tale of Atrahasis has been theorized to have been written by followers of Enki and therefore cast him in a benevolent light while making Enlil seem like a petulant tyrant. The shades of history are only as transparent as the person who is recording it.

# Chapter 3 The Epic of Gilgamesh

Before we dive into the general myths and stories, we must make an important note. The myths do not always fit together nicely. Often, what happens in one myth directly contradicts something that happened in another. The names of gods frequently change, sometimes even during a single myth. The genealogy of the gods is convoluted with parents changing from one myth to another, making sisters into daughters and fathers into brothers. Gods who are married in one myth are married to other gods in a different myth. Gods killed in one myth are frequently resurrected to play a part in another story. Really, there is not much difference between them and modern-day soap operas! There is no real chronological order that events take place with the myths, so it is best if you just enjoy each story as its own entity. For readability, we have tried to stick to a single name for a god even if a different version was used in the text. Mesopotamian myths are very repetitious. This too has been streamlined for readability.

## The Epic of Gilgamesh

The most famous of all Mesopotamian lore is the oldest epic poem ever written. It predates Homer's *Odyssey* by about 1500 years, and many historians claim that Homer was greatly influenced by Gilgamesh's tale. The *Epic of Gilgamesh* was first told through oral tradition and stories before it was first recorded in cuneiform writing on clay tablets around 2100 BCE. Gilgamesh is believed to have been an actual King of Sumer and at some point after his reign of approximately 126 years, was lifted into god status by the Sumerian people. He even had a cult that worshiped him for a time, reinforcing his status as a deity.

Our story takes place after the great flood, the very same flood that is in the Bible and that Noah built the ark to survive. As we have seen, the flood is a common historical marker in Mesopotamian lore with their list of kings being broken into pre-flood and post-flood groupings. The flood marked a change in how humans and their gods interacted. Pre-flood there was much more mixing between man and the gods, and the gods took a more active role in the lives of men. Gilgamesh comes to power a couple of hundred years after the great flood, but the flood and the gods feature prominently in his story.

The following version of the epic primarily comes from the "standard" Akkadian version. Following the epic, some of the main differences between the Babylonian version and the standard version are highlighted. There are also some Sumerian poems that parallel and augment the epic included.

The *Epic of Gilgamesh* was actually written in retrospect of Gilgamesh's life after he entered into the twilight of his life. It was supposedly written by Gilgamesh himself as a kind of memoir. It commences with a recitation about Gilgamesh's many accomplishments throughout his life.

Born of the goddess Ninsun and the third king of Uruk, Lugalbanda, Gilgamesh was two-third god and one-third human. (The math does not really work out, but the goddess apparently created him through divine magic, so traditional math may not apply!) With his demigod status, Gilgamesh was far above the average man – in *every* way according to the poem. A mountain of a man, he was taller and broader than any other man, and his strength was legendary. He had traveled the known world and had recovered the knowledge that had been lost in the flood. It was said that he knew all there was to know, including the mysterious and the hidden secrets of the world. As a warrior, he was unparalleled, equally able to lead the vanguard or protect the rear flank. As King of Uruk, he raised the walls again, built temples to please the gods, and made Uruk strong. No other man could claim, "I am King," like Gilgamesh.

Now that we have established that Gilgamesh was a great and mighty king, let us set the stage for the actual story. It begins in Uruk, a city-state of Sumer that sat on banks of the ancient path of the Euphrates. The city was permeated by canals and had a sophisticated infrastructure for the time. Gilgamesh was one of the early kings of the city, probably the fourth or fifth ruler. The city had been sacked and reclaimed several times during its early existence, and when Gilgamesh came to power, it was in a bit of a sorry state. The walls were down, and several of the temples had been destroyed.

Unfortunately, Gilgamesh, as a young man, was not a good king, or even a good man. He fought with his warriors for the simple pleasure of beating them. It was said that no maid in his kingdom went to her bridegroom without Gilgamesh first taking his pleasure with her. In short, Gilgamesh was a tyrant.

The people of the city cried out to the gods to make their king stop his brutal, heavy-handed ways. They called Gilgamesh the Wild Bull because his mother was the Wild Cow Goddess. However, when the people complained to the gods about his behavior, they said that Gilgamesh was lording his power over the city like an unrestrained wild bull amongst a flock of sheep.

The gods were displeased with this behavior and abuse of power by Gilgamesh. They believed Gilgamesh should be a shepherd to his flock and not a brutal overlord. Anu, the mightiest of all the gods, summoned Aruru, the Mother Goddess, and creator of mankind. Anu bade her to create a man who was equal in strength and power to Gilgamesh and who would be able to match the storm of Gilgamesh's heart. The man was to go to Uruk, challenge, and hopefully, humble Gilgamesh into giving up his tyrannical ways.

And so, after cleansing her hands, Aruru took a pinch of clay and cast it into the wild. She created the mighty Enkidu, known as the "hero and offspring of silence." Ninurta, the god of farming, healing, law, and war, lent his power to make Enkidu strong and solid.

Enkidu knew nothing of people or their ways when he was placed on the Earth. Wild and completely ignorant, his body was covered in thick matted hair, and the hair on his head was long and wild like a woman's. He grazed with a herd of gazelles and went to the watering hole where he enjoyed the company of all sorts of different animals.

One day at the watering hole, the trapper's son saw Enkidu. After seeing Enkidu at the watering hole two more times in as many days, the hunter told his father about the wild man. Enkidu had been causing the hunter much trouble. Every hole he dug to lay a trap, Enkidu filled in. Every snare he set, Enkidu took down. Every time he caught an animal, Enkidu set it free. The hunter was frustrated but also very scared of the wild man. Enkidu's strength was unmatched, like that of a rock from the sky, and he was obviously a child of the wild and knew nothing of the ways of men.

The hunter's father listened to his tale and then told his son, "Go to Uruk and seek out mighty King Gilgamesh. He is the only one with enough strength to best the wild man." His father also instructed him to find the harlot, Shamhat. She was known to be the most beautiful and alluring woman in Uruk. His father knew that she would be able to tempt the wild man and once he succumbed to her charms, the beasts would not allow the wild man to stay among them.

So, the son made haste for Uruk. He sought out King Gilgamesh and told him the story of the wild man. Then he proposed his father's plan, which Gilgamesh fully supported. He commanded the hunter to find Shamhat and take her to the wild man where she should remove her clothes and lure Enkidu to her.

The hunter soon found Shamhat, and they set out for the wilderness. After three day's journey, they arrived at the waterhole, and the wait began. After two days of waiting, Enkidu finally came to the watering hole. The hunter told Shamhat to take off her clothes and entice Enkidu to her. The hunter encouraged Shamhat, "Oh, beautiful lady. Take in his scent and let him lie atop you. Do for the man the work of a woman."

Shamhat bravely stood her ground as Enkidu caught sight of her and came to her as a man comes to a woman. This took tremendous courage since Enkidu was more animal than man, covered in hair, with no words or knowledge of the ways of man.

Shamhat took him to her and for a week held him in her embrace. Once Enkidu's desires had been quenched, he raised his head and looked around him. The animals withdrew from him in fear as he now was more man than animal. He tried to run after them and found that he could no longer run as swiftly as an antelope. He did, however, understand why they ran and understood the ways and reasons of man.

Enkidu returned to Shamhat and studied her face and features as she spoke to him. Shamhat told Enkidu that he was as beautiful as a god. She asked, "Why do wander among the beasts of the wild? Come with me to Uruk and live among the people there. I will take you to the temple of the great god Anu and goddess Ishtar." Then, she told Enkidu about the tyranny of Gilgamesh and begged him to deliver her people from his brutality.

Enkidu agreed to go with her, instinctually feeling that this was the path he was to take. He felt compelled to seek out a worthy friend and comrade. He said, "I will go to Uruk and the temple of the great god Anu and goddess Ishtar. I will challenge and best Gilgamesh, and it will be known that I am the mightiest of all. I will set order to Uruk, and all will know the strength of a wild man!"

Shamhat told Enkidu of the wonders of Uruk – the festivals and beautiful women. Most of all she told him about Gilgamesh and how handsome and strong he was. Shamhat explained that Gilgamesh was favored by the mightiest of the gods. Anu, the supreme ruler of the gods, Enlil, the god of kings and the fates, and Ea, the god of the sea, all blessed Gilgamesh with great wisdom, strength, and knowledge. The god Shamash, a sun deity, also particularly favored the king. Shamhat felt that Gilgamesh was the only man in the world worthy to be Enkidu's friend and comrade.

Shamhat told Enkidu that Gilgamesh had been having dreams about Enkidu's coming to Uruk. Gilgamesh shared his dreams with his mother, the goddess Ninsun. In the first dream, Gilgamesh said that he saw the stars in the heaven appear before him, and one fell from the sky and landed next to him. Gilgamesh was unable to pick it up or move it all. It was too heavy. The people of Uruk milled about it and seemed to revere it by kissing its feet and embracing it. Gilgamesh felt drawn to it, and this time, he was able to pick it up. He laid it at his mother's feet, and from it, she made Gilgamesh an equal. Ninsun heard her son's dream and of course, knew all about Enkidu. She told Gilgamesh that soon a man was coming that would be his savior and comrade in all things.

The second dream was very similar. Gilgamesh explained to Ninsun that in this dream, he saw an ax in the middle of the city of Uruk. Again, the people surrounded it. Gilgamesh picked up the ax and was inclined to it to hold and embrace it as a wife. Like the first dream, he placed it at the feet of his mother, and she created an equal for Gilgamesh. Ninsun, in her wisdom, told her son that the ax symbolized his soon-to-be friend and comrade. She said that his comrade would save him many times and would have the strength of a rock from the sky.

Shamhat explained that Gilgamesh took great joy in the dreams and was eagerly awaiting his comrade. He knew that Enlil, the god of fate, had decreed that he would have a friend and advisor. Despite Gilgamesh's apparent eagerness, Shamhat and Enkidu tarried in the wilderness a bit longer to enjoy each other's company before starting their journey to Uruk.

Finally, Shamhat took Enkidu to a shepherd's camp. She used some of her clothing to cover his nakedness and brought him to the shepherds as if she were presenting a god to them. They took in his mighty strength and build and knew that he must be the man from Gilgamesh's dream. The shepherds gave him bread and ale, but Enkidu did not know what to do with them. Shamhat showed him what to do with the food and drink, and Enkidu ate his fill of bread and no less than seven tankards of ale. Enkidu, not used to alcohol, was fairly drunk after that much ale and began to sing and be merry.

The shepherds took him to the barber who shaved the hair from his body and trimmed back the hair on his head. He combed oil through his hair, and the shepherds clothed him in the garments of a warrior. After their ministrations, he looked a proper Sumerian warrior in all manner. The shepherds lay down and slept, leaving the mighty warrior, Enkidu, to watch their sheep. Enkidu single-handedly fought off wolves and lions to protect the flock while the shepherds slept the night away.

A man came upon Enkidu in the night, and Enkidu asked him where he was going. The man told him that he was bound for Uruk to serve the food at a wedding banquet. He told Enkidu of the custom that Gilgamesh practiced of taking the bride to his bed first before allowing her to go to her husband. Enkidu did not approve of this and headed straight away, accompanied by Shamhat, to Uruk to intervene.

The wedding festival was in full swing when Enkidu and Shamhat arrived in Uruk. The people stared at Enkidu and whispered about his strength and might. They knew this stranger must be the prophesied wild man come to save them from Gilgamesh's abuses. They surrounded him and kissed his feet, just like in Gilgamesh's dreams.

Gilgamesh was on his way to the bridal chamber, but Enkidu blocked the door and forbade him entry. Gilgamesh was infuriated, and he and Enkidu fell into combat in the city's streets. The battle was ferocious, and the walls shook with its violence. The warriors were evenly matched, but eventually, Gilgamesh gained a slight advantage. Enkidu acknowledged Gilgamesh's superiority and his destiny, blessed by Enlil, to be king. The fight ended, and the two men embraced as friends.

Gilgamesh took Enkidu to meet his mother, the Wild Cow Goddess, Ninsun. She was pleased to see her son with his fated companion. Gilgamesh extolled Enkidu's strength and stature among men. Ninsun said that was a shame that Enkidu had no family, no brother, or kin of any kind. Enkidu, who had never given this much thought before, was suddenly terribly depressed by the notion that he was all alone in the world. His strength left him, and he cried while Gilgamesh tried to comfort him.

Finally, Gilgamesh decided that what Enkidu needed was an adventure to perk him up. He decided that they would go to the great Cedar Forest and battle the demon Humbaba, who was the guardian of the sacred forest. Enkidu told Gilgamesh that it was not a good idea. He reminded his friend that Enlil had fated that Humbaba was to protect the forest. Enkidu knew of the Forest of Cedars from his time wandering with the herds in the uplands. No animal would go near the forest, including Enkidu. It was 60 leagues of enchanted land ruled by Humbaba, who had a voice as mighty as the Great Flood and words like fire. Humbaba's breath brought death to any who felt it. "No, my friend," Enkidu told Gilgamesh, "we do not need to go willingly into Humbaba's deadly ambush. It would be certain death."

Gilgamesh, in his typical kingly fashion, ignored his friend's counsel and simply said, "I will climb the slopes of the forest," and began his preparations for his quest to the Cedar Forest. Enkidu tried to dissuade Gilgamesh. He reminded him over and over about Humbaba's powers. He told Gilgamesh that they would be beset by tremors if they walked into Humbaba's forest. He pleaded with Gilgamesh, saying that Humbaba's wrath was second only to the thunder god Adad's mighty thunder.

Finally, in a last ditch effort to dissuade Gilgamesh from his ill-fated expedition, Enkidu said, "None of the gods dare challenge the demon Humbaba! Who are we to poke such a hornet's nest when the mightiest of gods would not attempt it?"

Gilgamesh had grown tired of his friend's nagging. He snapped at Enkidu, "Why are you being such a coward? You are a child of the wild. Men have fled from your presence, and even the lions fear you. You are a warrior, tried and true. Stand up and embrace our destiny, for we are more than mere men!"

With this rousing speech, Gilgamesh led the way to the blacksmith's forge. There, he commissioned hatchets to be made for their quest. They were given great axes and hatchets. The blacksmiths also created daggers for the warriors with golden hilts. All the weapons were massive and far more than any ordinary man could wield.

Once they were kitted out and ready for battle, Gilgamesh gathered the Uruk Council of Elders and his warriors and told them of his plan to kill Humbaba and bring back cedars from his forest. The warriors urged Enkidu to talk some sense into Gilgamesh. Gilgamesh again shrugged off his friend's advice, acknowledging the danger and the fact that he did not know what he was walking into.

Gilgamesh said, "I will make my name ring for all eternity with my victory. Upon my return, we will have a celebration that will be like celebrating New Year's twice over!"

The Council of Elders was not keen on the idea either. They told Gilgamesh that he was young and impetuous. They echoed every one of Enkidu's cautions. Gilgamesh only laughed, looked at his friend, and said sarcastically, "Oh, now I am so frightened! Should I run and hide?"

The Elders realized that Gilgamesh was set on his quest and that he would not be dissuaded. So, they changed tack and began to offer advice. They counseled Gilgamesh not to rely solely on brute strength to win the day. They encouraged him to be clever and wait to strike the blow that would be the most effective. Then they turned to Enkidu. "We trust our King to you. You shall take the lead and keep the king from harm. Bring him home to his wives," they instructed the young warrior.

Gilgamesh was in high spirits and led his friend to his mother to get her advice and blessing before they left on their quest. Ninsun was not pleased to hear her son's plans to conquer Humbaba. Ninsun retired to her bath to cleanse herself so she could make an offering to Shamash. Seven times she bathed in water scented with soapwort and tamarisk, and then, she made her way to the roof to offer her prayer.

She sat up an offering of incense and cried out to the sun god, Shamash, "Why have you touched my son and placed a restlessness in his spirit? He is going to fight that which you hate most, the evil forest spirit, the one second only to Adad. You must watch over him as he goes to slay Humbaba! Oh, great

Shamash, you bless the lands with your glow and make the plants and animals grow. Watch of my son, Gilgamesh. Make the days long and the nights short as he travels. Help his strides be true and his courage never falter.

"On the day of battle, rise up, Oh Shamash, the winds of East, West, North, and South. Bring the tempest and the hurricane down on Humbaba so that his face is darkened, shadowed from your light. Let Gilgamesh's weapons find their mark. Turn your radiance to your faithful follower.

"Glory shall be to you with the victory of Gilgamesh! Your brothers, the gods, will praise you with a feast and Aya the bride will comfort you and wipe your brow!

"Shamash, oh great God of the Sun, remember that Gilgamesh is destined for more! Is he not to rule the heaven at your side? Is he not to gain the wisdom of Ea and live with Ningishzida in the Netherworld?

"Do not forsake my son, oh Shamash! Bless his journey and return him safe to me!"

Once Ninsun finished her prayer, she returned to her son and his friend. However, it was not Gilgamesh she summoned to her side but Enkidu. To Enkidu, she said, "You did not come from my womb and are not of my blood, but know that from this day, you and Gilgamesh shall be brothers. Your way lies with his." She decorated his neck with symbols and embraced him. "You are my son and shall be one in brotherhood with Gilgamesh! Let your stride be true and your courage never falter. Protect your brother!"

With Ninsun's blessing, the warriors left to make their own preparations. They made offerings to Shamash and asked for his blessing and protection. Then, Gilgamesh turned his attention to the running of the city in his absence. He left instructions with the Elders, and Enkidu and he made to leave the city. The people ran behind them shouting encouragement. Above all, they reminded the warriors to strike true and let Enkidu take the lead. Enkidu followed Gilgamesh out of the city with the weight of responsibility heavy on his shoulders. He asked Gilgamesh one more time to turn back, but his request fell on deaf ears.

The two friends began their journey. The journey took six days. Every night, they dug a well and Enkidu made a dream house for Gilgamesh. There he made an offering of grain to the Dream God and invoked the mountain to send him a sign about their upcoming adventure. Gilgamesh slept, and Enkidu watched over him.

Every night, Gilgamesh had a dream which he shared with Enkidu and asked him to give him counsel as to their meanings. The first dream Gilgamesh said was full of chaos, but a mountain fell into the valley. He was fearful that the mountain symbolized Humbaba and showed his defeat. However, Enkidu assured him that this was not the case. He said that the dream was a good omen and that the mountain was not Humbaba, for how could it be when they were going to triumph over the demon and leave his corpse on the battlefield.

The second dream involved a mountain as well. This time the mountain held Gilgamesh fast by the feet, and he could not move. Then, he saw a stranger approach him. The stranger was the most beautiful person Gilgamesh had ever seen. The stranger freed Gilgamesh from the mountain, gave him water, and calmed his fears. Again, Enkidu assured Gilgamesh that the mountain was not Humbaba and Gilgamesh needed to cast aside his fears.

On the third night, Gilgamesh dreamed of a fierce storm that tore through the heavens. The Earth trembled as the day went dark. Lightning seared the night, and fires broke out all around. Then, death rained from the sky, quenching the fires and leaving everything in its wake a smoldering cinder. Enkidu offered another positive interpretation of the dream. He told Gilgamesh that he was the Wild Bull and it was his fury that shook the heavens. Enkidu said Gilgamesh would soon lock his horns into Humbaba, who could never stand against the Wild Bull. A dream such as this had to be a good omen of their victory.

Gilgamesh's fourth dream showed a monstrous thunderbird that flew around breathing fire and death. A man that Gilgamesh had never seen before materialized and pulled the great bird from the sky. He placed it at Gilgamesh's feet. Enkidu again found a way to see this dream as a good omen. He told Gilgamesh that they would bind Humbaba's arms and cast him down. He interpreted the man as the god, Shamash, and said that Shamash would deliver them in their time of peril.

The fifth and final dream involved an enormous bull. The bull caught Gilgamesh up on his horns. Again, the stranger appeared and pulled Gilgamesh free. He revived Gilgamesh with water from his waterskin. Gilgamesh woke from this dream completely distraught. Faithful Enkidu was there to support him. Enkidu told Gilgamesh again that the man in the dream could only be Shamash and that he would protect them in their quest.

Finally, they drew nigh to Humbaba's forest, and Gilgamesh's courage began to falter. Enkidu reminded him that he was the offshoot of the great city of Uruk and a mighty king. They had the blessing of Shamash and Ninsun and were about to make their names known for eternity. "Have heart, my friend. We are mighty warriors and have the protection of the gods. We cannot fail," Enkidu rallied his friend's courage.

Gilgamesh cried out in prayer to Shamash to protect him. Shamash called down an answer urging the warriors to make haste. He told them that Humbaba was only wearing one of his seven cloaks of protection at the moment and was vulnerable. It would be their best opportunity to beat the demon.

Humbaba felt them coming close to his forest and let out a terrible bellow. It shook the ground and made the men tremble. This time, it was Enkidu's courage that failed. He begged Gilgamesh to turn back and to flee. Gilgamesh was having none of it. He said, "Are you not a warrior? Will you flee like a weakling? Stand strong on your legs and cease your trembling. Forget death and fight for life! Sound your battle cry and take my hand, for today we make our names ring across all eternity!"

And with that, the warriors entered the great Cedar Forest.

At first, all they could do was stand and marvel at the magnificent towering trees. The Cedar Forest was the forest of the gods and was vast and beautiful to behold. No mortal man was welcome there. The path that Humbaba walked through the trees was clear for them to see, but they did not want to travel too deeply into the forest. So, Gilgamesh and Enkidu drew their axes and chopped down one of the sacred trees.

As they had hoped, Humbaba appeared almost instantly. He sneered at the two men, calling Gilgamesh rude and brutish. He insulted Enkidu, calling him the spawn of a fish and hatchling of a turtle. He was particularly angry with Enkidu. Humbaba had seen Enkidu as a wild man and had not bothered him. Now, Enkidu had brought Gilgamesh to his forest to take his sacred trees, and Humbaba felt betrayed. "I will slit your throat and feed your flesh to the birds, Enkidu," Humbaba taunted.

Gilgamesh watched in horror as Humbaba's face became a gruesome mask. He turned to Enkidu in fear and said, "I'm not sure this was such a good idea! Do you see how he changes? Do you see his power?"

Enkidu used Gilgamesh's words back at him. "Are you not a warrior? Are you a weakling? Your talk makes me sick! Now is the time for action. It is too late to turn back! Make your blow strike true!"

And with that encouragement, Gilgamesh and Enkidu leapt into battle with Humbaba. As they fought, the earth burned beneath their feet, and the clouds turned from white to black. It rained death down on them as a gray mist. Shamash remembered his promise to Ninsun and called the thirteen winds to bind Humbaba. Humbaba's face grew dark and angry, but he could not move. Gilgamesh held his ax to the demon's throat. Humbaba begged for his life, "If you let me live, I'll give you as many trees from the forest as you like. From now on, I will guard the forest for you, and you will be my king."

Enkidu urged his friend not to listen to Humbaba and make a quick end of it. He knew that the gods would not be pleased when they heard of the deeds that they had done, for it was the sacred forest and not the forest of men. They needed to finish this business and leave quickly.

Humbaba spat at Enkidu, "I should have hung you from a tree when I had the chance! But, Enkidu, tell Gilgamesh to spare my life. He will listen to you!"

Enkidu was not swayed by Humbaba's pleas. He said to Gilgamesh, "Be done with this! Banish his magic and be quick before Enlil hears of this! Hurry and make your name – Gilgamesh the one who slew the ferocious Humbaba!"

Humbaba was not one to give up easily. "Enkidu, you are like a servant to Gilgamesh, but you have the power to release me! Say the word and stay Gilgamesh's hand!"

Enkidu was increasingly worried that the gods were going to notice the disturbance in the Cedar Forest. "Gilgamesh, you must strike now before the gods descend in anger! Strike and become the hero that killed the forest demon Humbaba!"

Humbaba saw that Enkidu would not help him and he cursed him. "Neither of you will grow old. Enkidu, Gilgamesh will bury you, and you will know no peace in this life!"

Enkidu was frightened by the curse and at last, succeeded in prodding Gilgamesh into action. "He has cursed me! Cut off his head before he can do more!"

With a mighty swing of his blade, Gilgamesh cut off Humbaba's head. Enkidu pulled out his lungs, for good measure. They claimed the demon's tusks as their prize.

In the aftermath of the battle, the two friends explored the forest, and Enkidu told Gilgamesh to take what trees he wanted. When Gilgamesh voiced his uncertainty about it, Enkidu said, "You are the hero and have banished the demon. Who is going to question what you do?"

With that advice, they chose a great cedar to take back to Uruk to make a mighty door for the Temple of Enlil. They built a raft, and with the cedar in tow and Humbaba's head in a bag, they made their way down river to Uruk.

Once they returned to the city, Gilgamesh went straight to the palace and cleaned his weapons and then, himself. His long sojourn in the wild had left him a mess. Finally, clean and wrapped in fine linen, he donned his crown.

The Lady Ishtar, goddess of love and sexuality, looked on him and was taken with his beauty. She pleaded with the great king, "Oh Gilgamesh, will you be my husband? Please allow me to be your wife! I will harness the finest chariot of lapis and gold, and you will drive it to our house behind a team of lions and giant mules. I will kiss your feet, and the nobles and courtiers will bow and kneel before you. I will bless your house and your livestock. Your goats and sheep will be fertile; your donkeys will be swift no matter how laden with burden, and your horse will never be beat."

Gilgamesh replied, "And, my Lady Ishtar, will you provide food and ale fit for a king? I doubt it! You are like a frost that does not freeze or a door that neither allows a breeze in or out. You are a sticky residue that stains the hand. You are a waterskin that cuts the hand of the drinker. You are weak limestone in a mighty wall of ashlar. You are a shoe that bites the foot within it! When have any of your lovers endured forever? When have any of the mighty warriors that you have taken to your bed found their glory in heaven?"

Gilgamesh plowed on, not sparing the lady's feelings. "Your love is poison, Ishtar. You loved the beautiful speckled bird, but you struck it down and broke its wing. Flightless now, he stands crying in the forest. You loved the lion for his perfection and strength but dug holes to trap him in the earth. Your love for the horse brought him under saddle and whip to be doomed to drink muddy water." Gilgamesh ignored Ishtar's tears. Steadily, he laid out the sad picture of those who had felt the tainted love of Ishtar.

49

"And what of the shepherd, who showered you with gifts? You turned him into a wolf! Now, he is spurned by his own boys, and his dogs bite at him! And of course, let us not forget your father's gardener! He brought you treats of nuts and dates, and you asked him to lie with you. He was no fool and refused you. But you could not allow that! You cursed him into a dwarf and sentenced him to continue in his labors without ceasing!" Gilgamesh turned away from the goddess, saying, "So, no, my Lady Ishtar, please do not share your love with me!"

Ishtar was mortified and furious with Gilgamesh for embarrassing her. She flew to the sky to find her father, the great Sky God Anu. Ishtar ranted and raved about the insult she had been paid. She cried at her father's feet saying she had been scorned and slandered.

Unperturbed by his daughter's hysterics, Anu simply shrugged and said, "You started the whole thing by pushing yourself upon him, Daughter. You have none to blame for this but yourself."

Ishtar's fury boiled over. "I will have vengeance! Give me the Bull of Heaven. With him, I will make Gilgamesh pay for his hateful words!" When her father hesitated, she added, "If you do not do this – if you don't give me the Bull of Heaven to exact my revenge, I will lay waste to the gates that bind the Netherworld. I will raise the dead. They will spill forth and consume the living."

Faced with the very real danger of the first zombie apocalypse, Anu tried to reason with his daughter. "The Bull of Heaven will not only wreak havoc on Gilgamesh, but the people of Uruk will suffer as well. You may have the Bull, but only once every widow in the village has set aside seven years of provisions."

Ishtar assured her father it was already done. With no other reason to deny her, Anu handed her the great bull's rope that would pull him down from the heavens.

Ishtar left the sky, leading the Bull of Heaven, Taurus, behind her. The moment his massive hooves touched the ground, the fertile reed beds withered and died. The great Euphrates dropped dangerously low. The beast snorted and stamped, and a huge trench formed in the ground, swallowing a hundred men of Uruk. Looking around, the Bull stomped his foot again, and the ground gave way to swallow two hundred men. With a third snort, the bull churned the ground beneath his feet, causing earthquakes and landslides.

Enkidu fell part way into the pit. With a tremendous leap, Enkidu jumped out and grabbed the giant bull's horns. Enkidu and the bull stared at each other, and the bull snorted and slobbered over Enkidu's face. He held on tight and called out to Gilgamesh, "We returned to the city heroes and here is a test of our strength! The Great Bull is strong, but together we can beat him. I will grab him by the tail and hold him still. You must swing your blade with the true aim of a butcher and kill him with a single stroke!"

In a single, swift motion, Enkidu let go of the bull's horns and vaulted over the animal to grab its tail. As he held tight, Gilgamesh, with his skillful aim, cut the beast's throat. The Bull of Heaven fell to the ground dead.

Gilgamesh and Enkidu cut out its heart and carried it as an offering to Shamash, who appeared before them to accept their offering. The men fell down on their knees and worshipped their god. When Shamash left them, they sat together in silence for a time.

Then, they heard Ishtar wailing from the walls of the city. "What has happened? Gilgamesh, the one who slandered and insulted me, has killed the Bull of Heaven!"

Enkidu stood and faced the wrathful goddess. Tearing off a haunch of the dead bull, he flung it high on the wall, hitting her in the face. He taunted her, "If I had the chance, I would do the same to you! You would hold your guts in your arms when I was through with you!"

Ishtar led the women of the city in mourning as fitting for such a noble beast while Gilgamesh and the men admired the mighty horns that were now the king's trophies. They proceeded to the palace where Gilgamesh asked his serving women, "Who is the mightiest of all warriors?"

The people raised a cheer to assure their king that there was none finer man than him. They made lavish offerings to the gods and cleansed themselves in the river. Spirits ran high, and a huge celebration ensued in the castle.

Later that night as the men were abed, sleeping the sated dreams of warriors, Enkidu had a dream of death and doom. In the morning, he went straight to Gilgamesh to tell him of his nightmare. "I dreamt the gods were in counsel one with another. The three mightiest of all the gods, Anu, Enlil, and Ea, were in discussion. Shamash, our protector, was there amongst them. Anu told them that because we had killed the great Bull of Heaven and the devil Humbaba that one of us must die! Enlil was quick to say that you, Gilgamesh, should live, and it was I that was to pay the price. Shamash, the radiant one, spoke on my behalf. He said that everything that had happened was at the word of Enlil, the controller of the fates. He said that we should not be punished for what Enlil had decreed, but Shamash's words were turned away since he had been our comrade and protector."

Enkidu fell to Gilgamesh's feet and wept, the weight of his impending doom settling heavy upon him. "Oh Gilgamesh, my dearest brother, I shall know no mercy," Enkidu cried. "The gods will send me to my death, and I will sit among them in the darkness, never to see you, my brother, again!"

In his despair, Enkidu wandered the city until he came to the great door he had fashioned from the sacred cedar of Humbaba's forest. His tears wet the wood as he cried against it. "I know you are just a door of wood with no sense, but why have you not saved me? I sought you out in twenty leagues of forest and culled you carefully with my ax. Down the Great Euphrates, I floated you and crafted you in perfection for the temple of the Mighty Enlil. Did you bring me blessings? Nay! Death is what you brought me!" Enkidu pulled the door from its hinges and flung it down, weeping bitterly. "May the king that comes after me hate you as much as I do! May you be hung where you will never be seen again," Enkidu cursed the door.

Gilgamesh watched in horror as his friend defiled the temple. With tears on his face, he pleaded with Enkidu to stop. "Do you see what you have done? You will anger the gods further! Let me go and make an offering to our protector, the Great Shamash. I will kneel and pray to the mighty Anu that he will grant mercy on you! I will make a mighty offering of gold to the gods in your name. Do not despair!"

Enkidu would not be consoled. "Do not waste your time, brother. The Wise Enlil does not change his mind. He controls the fates, and his words do not reverse themselves. Save your prayers and your gold! Sometimes, men die before their time. Such is their fate."

Lost in his grief, Enkidu lifted his face to the sun and called out to Shamash. "The hunter who brought me away from my herd, who introduced me to the ways of man, let him not be as great as the hunters around him. Curse his profits and his income. Let the gods flee from any home he enters!"

Enkidu was not finished after he cursed the hunter but turned his vengeance on his first lover, Shamhat. "And the harlot, Shamhat, I call a curse down on you. You shall never know the delight of a family. Your finest garments will be ruined by the dirt. You shall be cast away from the young women and never have a table of bounty set before you. You sapped my strength in the wild. I was perfect, and you took it from me!" Enkidu raved toward the sky, continuing to curse Shamhat's name, saying, "Let any man drunk or sober strike you down. Let the briars and thorns tear at your feet. Let you never know prosperity again!"

The great Shamash heard Enkidu's fevered cries and answered him from the heavens. "Why do you curse the harlot? Did Shamhat not feed you, clothe you, and bring you to your brother, the mighty Gilgamesh? Fear not, for Gilgamesh will see you laid out in splendor. In honor, he will lay you to his left, and the mightiest in the Underworld will receive you and kiss your feet! The people of Uruk will mourn you but none more than Gilgamesh. His hair will mat, and he will wander in the wilds, lost in his grief!"

Enkidu heard Shamash's words. The swirling anger and grief in him settled and drained from his breast. He repented of his angry curses. Again, he lifted his voice in supplication to Shamash. "Hear my plea for the harlot Shamhat! Let her know the love of mighty rulers. Let them shower her with gold and treasures. Let no soldier spurn her and let them give her gifts of fine jewelry. Let a man whose wealth is high leave his wife for the love of Shamhat and let her live in prosperity!"

Having settled his soul with this blessing for Shamhat, Enkidu slept. When he awoke, he sought out Gilgamesh, for he had had another terrible dream.

"I stood between the echo of earth and the thunder of heaven. I beheld a man with terrible features. His face was drawn and angry like a thunderbird. His hands were the paws of a lion with claws like an eagle's talons. He grabbed me, holding my hair tightly in his clawed hands. I struck at him, but he danced away as light as the wind itself. In one swift blow, he laid me low, and I was crushed beneath him. I cried out to you to save me, but before you could, he transformed me into a dove. The creature tied my wings and bore me down into the darkness."

Enkidu continued his recitation, "Into Irkalla, the great cavern of darkness below, where our souls go to wait for eternity, he took me. Into that place from which none leaves, and there is but dry soil and clay to eat, I was taken to join others and dwell in darkness cloaked in our coats of feathers. I saw the kings of old, their crowns cast off and forgotten. They toiled to serve the great gods food and drink. I saw the Queen of Darkness, Ereshkigal, as her scribe read aloud to her. She looked at me and asked who had brought me to her chamber."

Enkidu's grief overwhelmed him, and he wept in Gilgamesh's arms, pleading with him not to forget all that they had been through together.

Gilgamesh was astounded by the vision his friend had seen. He watched helplessly as over the next twelve days Enkidu slowly weakened and wasted away. Enkidu called Gilgamesh to him and cried, "The gods are against me. I will not die in battle. Who will remember my name?"

With Gilgamesh at his side, Enkidu died.

Gilgamesh held his brother close and wept bitterly. "What sleep has gripped you? Wake up!" Of course, Enkidu was gone. Gilgamesh began his lament as the sun rose, bathing the city in the light of dawn.

With his face turned to the sky, Gilgamesh began, "Oh Enkidu, child of a gazelle, child of the wild! Let the paths of the Great Cedar Forest mourn your passing. Let the Elders and people of Uruk bless and mourn you! May the mountain peaks and the pastures lament your passing with motherly devotion." Gilgamesh went on invoking the beasts and the trees to mourn for Enkidu. He called upon every man in Uruk from the lowliest shepherd boy to the Elders of the city to raise their voices to mourn his brother. Finally, Gilgamesh proclaimed, "I mourn my brother; I weep from my friend! Despite my ax at my side, the dirk in my belt, my shield over my face, and my finest clothing – I have been robbed of something most precious! Oh Enkidu, who climbed mountains and fought by my side, I mourn you!"

At the end of his lament, Gilgamesh tenderly covered his friend's face with a shroud. In his grief, he paced about his rooms like a caged lion and tore at his hair. His ripped his fine clothes from his body in his agitation. As the city woke with the sun, he called out to the craftsman of the city. He ordered a statue of Enkidu of the finest gold and lapis to be built. He called for an extravagant bed to be made and filled it with gold and ivory from his own treasury. He paid lavishly for Enkidu's passage into the Underworld so that he would find favor with the rulers there. He slaughtered the finest sheep and oxen to feed the royalty of Irkalla. He fashioned specific gifts for the different deities who held power there.

For the mighty Ishtar, he made a gleaming throwing stick. For Queen Ereshkigal, he fashioned a flask from the precious lapis lazuli. A flute of gold was made for the shepherd of the gods, Dumuzid, and a lavish throne made of lapis for the god of death, Namtar. He even crafted jewelry for the sweeper, housekeeper, and butcher to ensure they cared for Enkidu's comfort.

Once the burial preparations were made, Gilgamesh sent his beloved Enkidu off to Irkalla in the finest style of the day. Enkidu was sealed in his tomb, and his spirit made the journey to the Underworld.

Gilgamesh was full of sorrow and pain. He left Uruk and began to roam in the wild. He thought bitterly of death and sometimes wished he could die too so that he could be at peace like Enkidu. That thought never lingered long, for his fear of death was too strong. He formed a vague plan that he would roam the wilds searching for Uta-napishti, the man the gods had made immortal.

Gilgamesh wandered day and night until he came to a pass in the mountains. He grew afraid when he saw lions guarding the pass and prayed to Sîn, the god of the moon, to keep him safe. He fell asleep only to wake in the light of the moon feeling very light of heart and safe. He knew that Sîn was watching over him and grabbed his ax. He killed the lions and ate them. He wore their furs as he continued to wander in the wilderness, chasing the winds.

The sun god, Shamash, began to worry about Gilgamesh and his aimless wanderings. He called down from his heavenly seat, "Gilgamesh, why are you wandering? You'll not find what you seek wandering alone in the wild."

Gilgamesh answered, "Will I not have plenty of time to sleep when I am in the Netherworld? I will enjoy the sun on my face while I can, for in the dark of death there is no light."

Gilgamesh's wandering continued until he found the twin peaks of Mashu that served as the gates to the Underworld. A pair of hideous scorpion men guarded the pass.

"He who is come has flesh of god and man," one of the scorpion men observed.

"Tell me how it is you have come here? The journey is long and perilous. We would hear your story," the other scorpion man commanded.

Gilgamesh retold his adventures to the two creatures and then said, "I am seeking Uta-napishti, the one who has cheated death. I must have his secret."

"Never has anyone tried to walk the path of these mountains," warned the guard. "Through the darkness, you must travel. Time moves slowly, and you will have not the faintest glimmer of light to show you the path."

"I have come too far to turn back because it is dark! I will pass over these mountains," Gilgamesh proclaimed.

The scorpion men stood aside to let him pass, saying, "Safe journey, King Gilgamesh! May the mountain grant you safe passage!"

So, into the mouth of the pass, Gilgamesh walked. Immediately, darkness engulfed him, and he could not see a glimmer of light behind or in front of him. He walked for hours upon hours in total darkness. Finally, he stumbled out into the blinding sunshine.

Gilgamesh looked around him in wonder. He was standing in a grove of trees that bore precious gems instead of fruit. He delighted in the beauty around him and took his time exploring the grove.

Unbeknownst to Gilgamesh, he was being watched. The ancient and wise goddess, Shiduri, who kept the tavern on the edge of the Underworld, observed him from a distance. She was not sure what to make of the part god, part man who wandered in grove cloaked in lion pelts and looking half-wild himself. Shiduri thought that he must be a mighty hunter and a very dangerous creature to have walked through the Forest of Darkness. As Gilgamesh began to make his way toward her, she decided that she wanted to know more about him before she let him into her tavern. She closed and barred her gate and fled to the rooftop of her tavern to wait.

Gilgamesh stopped at the gate and called up to Shiduri, "Tavern keeper, why did you close your gate and run from me? I will smash the gate to bits if you do not let me in!"

Shiduri called back from her perch on the roof, "You are a wild man that I know not! I will not come down and open my gate until you tell me about your journey here!"

Gilgamesh answered with sorrow in his heart, "I am the friend of the great Enkidu who, together with him, slew the demon Humbaba and the Great Bull of Heaven."

Shiduri wasn't convinced, for the man in front of her looked nothing like a great hero. "If you are the hero who slew Humbaba and the Great Bull, why do you look like a child of the wild? Why are your cheeks sunken and skin burnt? Why is sorrow etched so deeply on your face?"

Gilgamesh replied with a mournful tone, "How could I not have sorrowful features and sunken cheeks? Enkidu, my friend, and comrade has died a mortal's death. I sent him well into the kingdom of Irkalla, but my heart is broken. I despair my loss!" Gilgamesh looked at the woman on the rooftop and continued, "Tell me true, Tavern Keeper, where is the landmark to find Uta-napishti? Does it lie across the ocean? Tell me, and I shall go there straight away. If it does not exist, then let me wander back into the wild."

The Tavern Keeper shook her head. "There has never been a way across the ocean, Gilgamesh! Only the mighty Shamash can cross the ocean. And do not forget about the Waters of Death! If you manage to survive the perils of the ocean, how do you plan to survive the Waters of Death?" Shiduri saw that Gilgamesh was determined and so she said, "Go and find Urshanabi. He is the boatman for Uta-napishti. If anyone can help you on this foolish errand, it is he and his crew made of stone."

Gilgamesh didn't waste any time. He took up his ax and hastened to the forest. Like the wild bull he was named for, Gilgamesh charged into Urshanabi's camp with his ax raised. Urshanabi raised his ax to meet Gilgamesh's strike, but he was no match for the mighty warrior king. Gilgamesh pinned him down and knocked him out. The crew of the Stone Ones were scared and cowered. Gilgamesh in his battle fury smashed them for their cowardice and threw them in the river.

Urshanabi regarded Gilgamesh when he returned from the river and introduced himself, asking Gilgamesh's name as well.

Gilgamesh answered, "I am the man who has roamed the wild and walked the hidden road. I am Gilgamesh!"

Urshanabi looked at him and asked, "Why do you look so sad? What grieves you so that you wander in the wild all alone wearing the pelts of lions?"

Gilgamesh once again related his grief at losing Enkidu. Then he said to the boatman, "Tell me how to cross the ocean! Tell me the landmark for the road to Uta-napishti!"

Urshanabi shook his head sadly. "Gilgamesh, you fool! When you destroyed my Stone Ones, you destroyed your way across the ocean. However, there may be another way. Go to the forest and cut at least 300 punting poles. Bring them to me once you have finished, and we will see about crossing the ocean."

Without delay, Gilgamesh went straight to the forest and began chopping down trees. He made the required 300 punts to Urshanabi's specifications and brought them to the boatman.

Urshanabi checked the punts and decided that they would suffice. Together, he and Gilgamesh set off in his boat across the ocean. They traveled swiftly, making the month and a half journey in just three days. As they entered the Waters of Death, Urshanabi instructed Gilgamesh to push the craft across with the punting poles. "But, be careful, Gilgamesh," Urshanabi warned. "Do not touch the waters, for even a single drop will mean instant death!"

Gilgamesh steadily pushed the boat through the waters and went through all three hundred punting poles. They were still not to the other side of the Waters of Death. So, Gilgamesh and Urshanabi took off their clothes and made a sail from them. Gilgamesh held up his mighty arms and acted as a mast. The wind carried them slowly forward.

On the far shore, Uta-napishti stood watching and wondering who was coming in the boat. He recognized the boatman but worried about the absence of the Stone Ones. Most of all, he wondered who the unknown man was.

As the boat drew up to the shore, Gilgamesh dropped his arms and called out to Uta-napishti, "Are you Uta-napishti, the man with life eternal and the only man to survive the great flood?"

Uta-napishti regarded the stranger in the boat for a moment before answering. "I am Uta-napishti. Who are you with your sorrowful face? Why do wear the pelt of animals and look like a creature from the wild?"

"I am Gilgamesh, King of Uruk." He then told Uta-napishti about the loss of Enkidu and his grief. He told him about his wanderings and his plan to find the man with eternal life. "And so, here I am. I am ready to bar the door of sorrow and find happiness again! Please, set me free from my sorrows!"

Uta-napishti shook his head sadly at Gilgamesh. "Oh, mighty King Gilgamesh! You are part god and part man, a mighty king. Why do you chase sorrow? Have you ever compared yourself to the lowly fool? The fool who gets only rags to wear and scraps to eat? Your lot is not all that hard! Yes, the gods took Enkidu to his doom, but this is the way of life. All men die. It is fated. You should not waste the good life you have been given trying to change that which cannot be changed!"

Gilgamesh was not about to give up that easily. "I see you standing before me, Uta-napishti. You look like any other man, but you have cheated death. I came here prepared to take your secret by force, but now I find that I cannot raise my hand against you. Tell me, old one, how is it that you were granted life eternal?"

Uta-napishti decided to take pity on Gilgamesh. "Let me tell you a secret known to no other man." Gilgamesh listened eagerly as Uta-napishti told his story.

"On the banks of the great Euphrates, there was an old city called Shuruppak where the gods liked to dwell. The town was overflowing with people and was crowded, noisy, and filthy. The gods were displeased. There was an Assembly of the Gods, held in secret. It was there they decided to destroy the city with a flood. Father God Anu made the rest promise not to reveal the plan. My master, Ea, god of the sea, was loath to see the life he helped create be washed away. He whispered to the reed wall around my house and told me through it of the secret plan. He commanded me to build a boat and to bring all the living creatures aboard.

"I answered him through the reeds and told him that I heard and understood. I asked, 'But what am I to say to my countrymen when they ask me what I am doing? How do I answer them without revealing the secret?'

"Ea told me to answer thusly, 'Enlil is punishing me. I must go to live with my master below the seas. Fear not! You will be sent rains in abundance, and you will harvest riches beyond measure.'

"I began immediately on the boat. I hired craftsmen and set them to work. Within five days, the hull was built and divided into seven decks with nine compartments. We fitted a furnace and a roof to the vessel, and all the while, I fed the workers with fresh meat and let a river of wine flow for them. It was very hard work, and eventually, the boat was oiled and ready to be sealed for the journey.

"I brought on board all of my wealth, my family, and all of the living creatures as I had been commanded by the great God of the Sea. The sky grew dark and foreboding with Adad, the storm god, leading the tempest. He was born along on his throne by his servants Hanish and Shallut. Errakal, the god of destruction, was unleashed and uprooted mooring poles and wreaked havoc. Ninurta, the mighty god of war, flooded the levees while Anu, Enlil, and the others laid waste around them with flame and fire. As the fearsome Adad passed over, the stillness was absolute, but in his wake, the gale and storm began with a ferocity never known to man.

"The rain lashed down, and the floods began. Destruction and death were everywhere. The gods beheld what they had wrought and flew to heaven in fright. Ninmah, the mother goddess who had breathed life into all living things, wailed and tore at her hair as she watched the devastation unfold. She wept bitterly, crying, 'This is all my fault! I spoke evil in our meeting, and now, my children are like fish in the ocean! How could I have let this evil plan happen?'

"All of the gods joined her and wept and wailed over their hasty actions. For seven days the rains fell, and the floods rose, flattening the land and killing everything.

"On the seventh day, the seas calmed, and the tempest blew no more. I cracked open the hatch, and my heart was full of joy to feel the sunshine on my cheek. But my heart was heavy, for all my people were no more than clay. I sat and wept as all around me there was nothing to see but ocean. In the distance, I could see 14 points of land breaking the surface of the ocean.

"The boat ran aground against the top of Mount Nimush, and there we stayed for six long days. On the seventh day, I set free a dove, but I knew there was no land close when the dove returned, unable to land elsewhere. The next day, I let fly a swallow, but it too returned. Finally, on the tenth day after the seas had calmed, I turned loose a raven. The raven did not return, and I knew the waters were receding.

"I made an offering to the gods. The incense I burned drew them like a moth to a candle, for they had thought there was no one left to leave them offerings. Beautiful Ninmah, the Mother of All, was the first to arrive. She rejoiced and swore on her beads of lapis that she would never forget that moment. She called to the other gods to join her, except Enlil, who she felt was responsible for everything.

"Enlil did not stay away, however. He was furious when he arrived. 'How is this possible? Why is this man alive? Everyone was to perish!'

"Ninurta was quick to point out that it had to have been Ea who had told me the secret of the gods.

"Ea was also full of rage. He had not liked the plan from the beginning and lashed out at Enlil. 'You did this, Enlil, the Sage of the Gods! You didn't take counsel and took it upon yourself to make this happen. You could have chosen to set loose a lion or a wolf to rid the town of some of the people. You could have sent a plague or a famine. But you chose to destroy everything!' Ea's anger was terrible to behold. 'I did not share the secret. Uta-napishti saw it in a vision and has learned our secret. Now, Enlil, oh great Sage of the Gods, what will you do with him?'

"Enlil stood before me and bade my wife come to us. As we knelt before him, he touched us on our foreheads. He said, 'Uta-napishti was once a mortal man, but no longer! Now he and his wife are like the gods with life eternal. He shall go to the land where the rivers begin and live in secret, away from the world of man!'

"Enlil bore us here, and here we have been since that day," Uta-napishti finished his tale and regarded Gilgamesh. "And so, Gilgamesh, what Counsel of Gods will come together to bless you with life eternal? If you really want immortality, then you must stay awake for six days and seven nights. Do this to show you are truly worthy."

Gilgamesh didn't think that it would be too hard. He had been scourging himself for months by going without sleep. However, the moment he sat down, sleep overtook him.

Uta-napishti shook his head and said to his wife, "See how much he wanted his eternal life? He hasn't even stayed awake a day."

His wife made to wake the sleeping king, but Uta-napishti stayed her hand. "He will think we have tricked him. Bake a loaf of bread and put it next to him to mark every day he sleeps."

Once six loaves were lined up next to Gilgamesh's head, the first ones already dried up and some of the others covered in mold, Uta-napishti woke the king. "Why did you wake me up," Gilgamesh demanded. "I had only just fallen asleep!"

Uta-napishti shook his head at him and pointed out the loaves. "Do you not see your daily bread here, untouched and decaying? How many loaves are there?"

Gilgamesh saw the evidence, and his heart sank. "Oh, what am I going to do, now? Death is waiting for me at every turn!"

Uta-napishti turned to his boatman. "Urshanabi, you brought this filthy man here. You must take him and see him bathed and cleaned. Fit him in garments fitting his dignity. Then, return him home."

Urshanabi obeyed his master, and soon, Gilgamesh looked like the king he was. The two men climbed aboard the boat, and Uta-napishti and his wife stood on the quayside as they took their leave. Uta-napishti's wife said to her husband, "Gilgamesh traveled so far, and his journey was difficult. What is he taking away from his visit here?"

Uta-napishti thought for a moment and called out to Gilgamesh as he the boat started to slide away from the dock. "Gilgamesh, since you traveled so far, and your journey was so difficult, I will tell you one more secret of the gods. At the bottom of the ocean, deep in the depths, there lives a plant that looks much like a boxthorn plant. It has terrible thorns and will prick any who tries to pick it. However, if you can succeed in picking this plant, you will be restored to your youth!"

Gilgamesh didn't waste any time as soon as they reached the ocean. He tied rocks to his feet and dove into the ocean. In the depths of the ocean, he found the plant he sought, and despite the thorns, he pulled it from the sandy bottom. He cut the stones from his feet, and the ocean delivered him to the shore.

He held up his prize to Urshanabi. "This is the Plant of Heartbeat. Any who eats it will be made young again. I am going to give it to an old man in the city of Uruk. If he becomes young again, then I will take it, too."

They traveled the road to Uruk, stopping now and then to eat and rest. When Gilgamesh happened on a pool of clean water, he left the plant on the edge of the pool and went in to bathe. A serpent ate the plant while Gilgamesh was washing. The snake slithered away leaving his shed skin behind (which is why snakes still shed their skins to this day!).

Gilgamesh was distraught. He sat on the bank of the pool and wept. "Why have I suffered so? Why did I work so hard to come out with nothing? Only the snake, the dreaded ground lion, has come out with anything!"

Urshanabi and Gilgamesh finished their journey to Uruk. Gilgamesh took Urshanabi to the wall around the city, and they looked over Gilgamesh's kingdom. Gilgamesh sat down and wrote this tale, so his story would not be forgotten.

That ends the great *Epic of Gilgamesh*. However, there are other stories of Gilgamesh, but they are often difficult to plug into the chronology of the epic. It is easiest to treat them as stand-alone stories.

## Gilgamesh, Enkidu, and the Underworld

In the early days of creation, there was much chaos as the gods created, destroyed, and claimed their parts of the world. Ereshkigal, the Queen of the Dead, had been stolen by the dragon, Kur, and was damned to spend her existence in the Underworld, for no one, not even gods, can return from there. Her brother, Ea, god of the sea, tried to set things back in order and return his sister. There were mighty storms and a great tempest as the gods tried to sort themselves out.

During the storm, there was a lone tree on the banks of the Euphrates. It was being thrashed by the storm and was in danger of being uprooted. A good woman from Uruk saw the young tree and heeded the words of the Father God Anu and the Wise God Enlil. She rescued the tree and brought it to Ishtar's favored garden within the city.

Carefully, she planted it with her feet. Every day, she cared for it by watering it with her feet and therefore, ensuring the tree would have magical properties. The Hulab tree grew mighty in the garden. Ishtar wanted the wood to build a bed and a chair. Patiently, she waited while her faithful servant, the woman who rescued the tree from the storm, cared for the tree with her feet.

After ten years, the tree was enormous and was the most vibrant plant in the garden. However, a serpent, who was immune to magic, had taken up residence in the roots of the tree and tried to strike anyone who got close. In the limbs, a mother thunderbird had made a nest and had a feisty brood of chicks that she was incredibly protective of. On top of that, a demon, the maiden Lilith, had moved into the trunk. She sang happy, joyful songs that made Ishtar weep with frustration.

The tree grew and grew, but the bark would not split, indicating it was ready to be harvested. The creatures repelled anyone who got close to the tree. Ishtar despaired she would never get her new bed or chair, which would mean she would never come into her full powers as a goddess and Queen of Heaven.

One day, her brother, Shamash, the god of the sun, was in the city. Ishtar pleaded with him, telling him of her troubles with the tree. If she could rid the tree of its three unwelcome guests, she could make her bed and chair. Shamash refused to help her, saying he had better things to do and he didn't care if she had a bed or a chair.

Several years later, Gilgamesh came to the garden. Ishtar begged him to help her with her tree. She explained the situation and Gilgamesh, never one to turn down a challenge, agreed to help her.

He took up his ax and with a mighty swing, killed the serpent. The thunderbird and demon decided that they did not want to share the same fate as the snake, and they quickly vacated the tree. Gilgamesh pulled the tree from the ground and plucked off its branches. He gave the trunk to Ishtar to make her throne and bed. He made himself a mallet and ball as a reward.

Gilgamesh went to the city looking for sport with his new ball and mallet. The city lads were happy to play until they realized that Gilgamesh played much rougher than they were used to. Their mothers and sisters came to the streets to revive them with food and drink, and the lads complained bitterly about how hard it was to play with the young king. When they stopped playing for the night, Gilgamesh left his ball and mallet in the street, ready for the next day's games.

When he went to find his ball and mallet the next day, they were gone. He searched high and low. Finally, he realized that they had been taken into the Underworld as a result of the women's cry of outrage for the treatment of their young lads.

Gilgamesh wept with frustration and anger over losing his ball and mallet. He reached down with his hand and then with his foot, but they stayed just out of his reach in the Underworld. In the end, he mourned his loss by saying, "Oh, my good ball and mallet! I had not yet had enough fun with you! Who will go get my lost things from the Underworld?"

The ever-faithful Enkidu saw his friend weeping and hurried over to help. When he heard the problem, he told Gilgamesh that he would go and retrieve his things from the kingdom of Irkalla.

Gilgamesh was exceedingly grateful and tried to warn his friend of the potential dangers of going into the realm of the dead. "You must not dress in clean clothes or go smelling freshly anointed with oils for they will know that you are a stranger there and surround you. Do not throw things or hold a rod of cornel in your hand. They will know you do not belong if you do." Enkidu listened patiently to his friend's warnings as Gilgamesh continued, "Do not wear sandals as you will make the earth shake. Do not kiss or strike your wives or sons. Most of all, do not be lured in by the beauty of the Queen of the Dead. She lays with her breasts bare in mourning for her husband, the Bull of Heaven. Her nails are like talons, and she will shred you like a lion."

Enkidu, while he had appeared to listen, paid no heed to Gilgamesh's warnings. Every single thing he had been warned not to do, he did, and he did not return from the Underworld. After a week, Gilgamesh was beside himself with worry and knew that the Netherworld had claimed his friend.

He petitioned Enlil for help and told him the whole story. He begged Enlil to retrieve Enkidu from the Netherworld. Enlil turned Gilgamesh away. Next, Gilgamesh tried the mod of the Moon, Sin, but again was rebuffed.

Determined to get his friend back, Gilgamesh sought out Ea, the god of the sea and faithful friend to mankind. Once Gilgamesh told Ea his story, the god called for Shamash, saying "When you next open the Netherworld to release the sun for its daily journey across the heavens, bring forth Gilgamesh's faithful friend, Enkidu."

Shamash did as he was told and with the sunrise, Enkidu's spirit was brought back to the world of man.

Gilgamesh was overjoyed to see his friend. "Tell me about the Underworld," he demanded of Enkidu after they had greeted each other.

"Oh, Gilgamesh, it is truly terrible there! The man who passed from life full of joy wastes away there. He decays like a louse-riddled garment and becomes filled with dust like a crack in the floorboards." Enkidu's expression was grim as he told his friend about the horrors of the Underworld.

Gilgamesh was dismayed at the tales Enkidu told, but he was still immensely curious. He could not stop himself from asking question upon question. "What of the man with only a single son? Did you see him? And what about the other man with two sons?"

"The man with one son laments his fate and cries bitterly. The man with two sons sits quietly on two bricks and eats bread," Enkidu told him.

Gilgamesh was fascinated and asked about men with every number of sons up to seven. Enkidu answered, "The man with three sons drinks contentedly from a water skin slung on his saddle. The man with four sons has as happy a heart as if he had four fat donkeys. The man with five sons enjoys free passage to the palace and the comforts there. The man with six sons lives like a lord and has a light heart. The man with seven sons sits with the gods."

Gilgamesh listened and thought for a moment before asking, "And what of the man with no sons, with no heir to his name or property?"

Enkidu shook his head sadly, "He is wretched and eats only bread burned like charcoal."

Of course, Gilgamesh had more questions. "The eunuch? How does he fare?"

"He stands propped in the corner, utterly useless."

Gilgamesh next asked, "What about a woman with no children, whose womb was barren?"

"She is shunned, and no man will take his pleasure with her."

Gilgamesh pressed on, "What about the young man who never knew a wife or the young woman who never knew a husband?"

Enkidu answered, "I have seen them, too. The young man weeps as he braids rope that will never be finished. The young woman weaves a reed mat that is wet by her constant tears."

The Underworld sounded like a dreary and depressing place, but Gilgamesh's questions were still not answered. "Tell me, my friend, did you see the leper or the man with pellagra? What of the men who were killed in violence? How do they fare in the Kingdom of Darkness?"

Enkidu shuddered as he thought of these wretched men. "The leper is kept out of the city gates and shunned by all. The man with pellagra writhes like an ox being eaten by maggots. The man ripped apart by lions suffers in misery. The men who drown in the flood and fell from the roof are not healed, and they too writhe in agony."

Gilgamesh's inquiry continued asking about other types of men, and Enkidu answered him, "The man who was disrespectful of his parents, burns with thirst that can never be quenched. The man whose parents cursed him roams as a ghost without an heir. The heroes of battles are held and lamented by their parents and wives, and the man who dies before his time shares the beds of the gods. The man who has no burial goods is fed scraps and crusts of bread and shunned."

Finally, Gilgamesh asked about one last type of person. "Enkidu, what about the still-born babes who never knew their names? What is their place in Irkalla?"

At last Enkidu smiled and said, "They play on the table of the gods among the silver with gold cups full of syrup and ghee."

The tale ends here abruptly without indication of what happened to Enkidu after the lengthy question and answer session with Gilgamesh. This story is looked upon as an appendix to the epic. Some think it was written to explain the Underworld to Gilgamesh and prepare him for his future role as minor god and judge in the Underworld.

## The Death of Gilgamesh

"Oh, our great King Gilgamesh, the Wild Bull, is laid low in his bed, never to rise again. Our mighty warrior, who was never bested in combat and was perfect in strength will never rise from his bed." The people lamented their king. "Gilgamesh the wise, who vanquished wickedness and always spoke wisdom is on his deathbed, never to be released. He climbed the mountain, our Lord of Uruk, but he will never rise again!"

The people wept and wailed for their king, who was in the grip of a mortal fever. "He who had perfect strength cannot stand and cannot sit. He cannot eat and cannot drink. Our great King is like a fish snared in the net or a gazelle in a trap. He is caught in the embrace of Namtar, the one who chooses the dead. Namtar, with no shape or substance, has caught him and will never let him go!"

For six days, Gilgamesh languished in bed with sweat pouring off of him, poised on the brink of death. In his fevered dreams, Enlil, the god of the fates, showed Gilgamesh a vision. Gilgamesh beheld the Assembly of Gods. To him, they said, "Gilgamesh, great King of Uruk, you have done many great things! You smote the demon Humbaba and carried away a precious cedar. You raised monuments and temples and made your city strong. You conquered the Waters of Death and sought out Uta-napishti in his home." Gilgamesh listened as the gods continued to extoll his achievements as King of Uruk. "You brought back the customs, rituals, and rites of ancient Sumer and

71

reinstated hand washing and mouth washing. This pleased us. You brought back the knowledge that was lost in the flood."

The gods discussed the fate of Gilgamesh between them. Anu, Enlil, and Ea all agreed, they had decided after giving Uta-napishti immortality that they would do it no more. Anu said, "Even though the goddess Ninsun pleads for her son's life, we cannot grant another mortal life eternal. Gilgamesh is only two-thirds god after all and therefore is still ruled by the laws of mortal man. Wise Enlil set his destiny to be that of a king and not a god, so death cannot be cheated."

Enlil and Ea supported Anu in his opinion, and Gilgamesh knew that he would not be granted immortality. He knew he was going to die. However, Enlil, the mighty god whose word determined the fates of man, decreed that Gilgamesh, while he would die a mortal death, would not live in the Netherworld like any other mortal.

Ea spoke to Gilgamesh, "You shall be the king of shades in the Netherworld. You shall sit beside Ningishzida and Dumuzid and pass judgment. Your word shall be as weighty as theirs, and you will have a chair among the Gods of the Darkness." Being among the gods of the Underworld would go a long way to making his stay there much more pleasant. However, Ea wasn't done. "Your way shall be lit by the goddess of dreams, Sissig. In your memory, Great King Gilgamesh, any warrior who wrestles during the Festival of Ghosts will also be given light, so the ghosts of their ancestors will be lit through the darkness of Irkalla."

These were great blessings and a large compromise for the gods. They clearly favored Gilgamesh and were trying to help him have the afterlife that they think he deserved. Enlil spoke to Gilgamesh in his dream. "Do not despair, Gilgamesh! Unknot your heart and be easy. You were born a mortal man and a mortal death you shall have. It is nothing to be saddened by! Besides, think of who you will meet there. Your father and siblings await you, and do not forget your faithful Enkidu! You will see them all and your rejoicing will be great!"

Gilgamesh awoke from his dream, blinking in the light. His heart was torn in two. On the one hand, he despaired because he knew his death was not far away. On the other hand, he was going to be lifted to a god once he left his mortal life. He asked himself if he wanted to act like a child and weep at his mother's knee and then reminded himself that he was the mighty king of Uruk. He sat up in his sick bed and bade his counselors come to him.

When his trusted counselors were around him, Gilgamesh told them of his dream. His counselors offered similar opinions to the god Enlil. "Mighty King, there has been no man yet to escape death. Does the bird leave the hand once it has been caught? Does a fish escape the net once it is caught? No man can escape the Kingdom of Irkalla once he has been called down into the darkness. Do not weep, oh Gilgamesh! There will never be another king as great as you! You are going to be a governor of the Netherworld and sit among the gods. What mortal has ever done that?"

Gilgamesh heard their counsel and accepted his lot, turning his attention to building his tomb. He was unsure as to where to put it, but Ea sent him a vision, solving his problem. When he awoke from his vision, Gilgamesh shouted for the craftsmen of the city to build dams and levees and divert the Euphrates. His tomb was to rest at the bottom of the river.

Anxious to please their king, the city folk worked hard and had the riverbed completely dry within a matter of days. Gilgamesh ordered the walls and door of the tomb to be fashioned from stone. The locks and hinges on the door were made from diorite, a hard granite type of rock. He made beams of gold to reinforce the inside of the structure. Then, he laid stones all about the bare riverbed to disguise the entrance of his tomb, so no one would ever be able to find it and raid it.

Into the tomb, Gilgamesh took his favorite wives and his trusted advisors. He arranged them as if they were at court. He sat out offerings for Ereshkigal, Queen of the Underworld, and the rest of the gods in her court. Finally, when all was just so, he laid down in his place, and the tomb was sealed.

The citizens of Uruk unstopped the mighty Euphrates, and the water washed over the tomb of their erstwhile king. They wailed and pulled their hair as they grieved his loss. The smeared themselves with mud and made offerings in the great Gilgamesh's name.

And thus ended the life and reign of King Gilgamesh.

## Babylonian Translations and Sumerian Poems

There are several tablets and fragments that offer slightly different versions of the Epic of Gilgamesh. This is probably the result of oral tradition and local customization of the story over the years. Depending on where and when the tablet was written, the story took on a slightly different flavor.

# The Ishchali Tablet

This tablet fragment deals with the slaying of Humbaba. The fragment begins with the capture of Humbaba. It is short, but the content is slightly different than the standard version.

Enkidu urged Gilgamesh to smite the demon. "What are you waiting for? Why don't you kill the demon ogre that is hated by the gods?"

"We must press our advantage. See how Humbaba's auras slip away into the forest? See how they grow dim? We should go after them," Gilgamesh replied.

Enkidu did not agree. "When a bird is caught in a snare, where do the chicks go? The auras will not go far. First, deal with the demon, and then, we will chase down the auras. Now, be done with this!"

Gilgamesh heeded his friend's counsel and, with a swing of his ax, beheaded Humbaba. The ravines ran with the blood of the ogre. The mountains trembled and quaked at the death of the Guardian of the Forest.

Enkidu and Gilgamesh started hunting down the auras. They found all seven of them and banished them. They also desecrated the forest, chopping the precious cedars. As they were laying waste to the forest, they came upon the secret lair of the gods.

The fragment ends here, but this is one of the first references to the "auras" of Humbaba.

## The Sippar Tablet

This fragment picks up after Enkidu's death, and Gilgamesh is on his quest for eternal life. Gilgamesh has wandered through the wilds and across the Forest of Darkness. He has come up the tavern keeper, Shiduri, and she has asked him why he was wandering with such a sorrowful heart.

"My beloved friend, Enkidu, has been taken by the mortal doom. He, who went with me and faced every danger, is no more. I held him close and wept for him. I kept hoping he would wake and rise up in answer to my cry. I waited seven days, as long as I could, until I saw a maggot drop from his nose. Then, I knew he would never rise again. I have wandered in the wilderness but have not found what I was seeking. Oh, Tavern Keeper, I do not want to die."

The Tavern Keeper answered the wretched Gilgamesh, "What are you wandering for, Gilgamesh? You are looking for what does not exist. When the gods made men, they made it their destiny to die and kept eternal life for themselves. But you are alive now, Gilgamesh! Go and live! Dance, sing, and be happy. Go and clean yourself up. Wear fine garments and wash your hair. Love your wife and children. They are the joy in life! Give up on this folly. Why keep searching for what you can never find?"

Gilgamesh did not want to hear the words of the Tavern Keeper. He replied, "Why do you say this to me, whose heart is broken? I miss my friend, Enkidu, too much to give up on my quest. You live here on the shores of the ocean. Tell me now, Tavern Keeper, how do I get across it!"

"Only Shamash travels across the ocean on his way to the Netherworld for his nightly slumber. However, there has never been another one like you, Gilgamesh!"

The fragment ends there. However, we assume that Shiduri tells Gilgamesh where to find Ur-shanabli and the Stone Ones to take him across the ocean.

# The Lord to the Living One's Mountain and Ho, Hurrah!

One of the longest poems that augments the epic is *The Lord to the Living One's Mountain* and *Ho, Hurrah!* This is a Sumerian poem that is about Gilgamesh and Enkidu's adventure to the Cedar Forest and the slaying of Humbaba. There are many differences in the stories, including the use of Bilgames or Gilgamec instead of Gilgamesh. For ease of reading, we will continue using the familiar Gilgamesh and refer to the gods by their Akkadian names that were used in the previous story.

We begin with Gilgamesh full of desire to establish his name and renown for all eternity.

"I will go the Cedar Forest. There I will be able to prove myself," Gilgamesh said to his faithful servant, Enkidu (in this version is most definitely a subordinate and not an equal to Gilgamesh).

Enkidu heard his master's desire to prove himself but urged caution. "I will leave with you right now for the Cedar Forest, but you should first seek a blessing of young Shamash, the sun god. It is to his domain you wish to go."

Gilgamesh heard the wisdom in the words and sacrificed a young goat to Shamash. He called up to the skies, "Please, hear me, oh Shamash. I wish to go to the mountains and seek the Cedar Forest!"

Shamash, his attention drawn by the offering, answered back from the heavens, "I hear you, but Gilgamesh, you are mighty within your own right. You are a king. What is in the mountains for you?"

Gilgamesh's eyes filled with tears as he pleaded to his God. "Please, Shamash! Look at my city. I see death all around me. I am a man and cannot escape death. I must go to the mountains so my name will be remembered!"

Shamash was moved by Gilgamesh's tears. "I will help you. Go to your city and find the men of a single mother. These seven brothers know all the routes of the earth. The oldest has paws of a lion with talons of an eagle. The second brother is a snake, and the third is a dragon. The fourth son burns with fire. The fifth brother is also a snake, and the sixth contains the waters of a flood. The seventh brother holds the power of lightning that no one can escape. These brothers will show you the way to the mountains and the forest you seek!"

Gilgamesh went to the great city of Uruk. He told all the men who had a household or a mother at home to go directly to them. From all the bachelors left in the streets, he called 50 of them to make an army to travel with him to the mountains. After a trip to the blacksmith to see his warriors properly outfitted, Gilgamesh, accompanied by Enkidu and the seven brothers, left Uruk with his band of 50 warriors to seek the Cedar Forest.

They traveled for a very long time. Over six mountain ranges, they followed the paths the brothers showed them, but Gilgamesh knew that none of the mountains held the sacred grove of cedars. Finally, they crossed into the seventh mountain range, and Gilgamesh knew they had found the right place.

When they found the cedar trees, Gilgamesh immediately began cutting the trees down with his axe. Enkidu and the others began cutting the branches off and putting them in a pile. The violation of his forest woke Humbaba, and he responded to the intruders by letting loose a terror, a kind of evil spirit, that put them all asleep.

Enkidu was the first to wake after having a terrible dream. He looked around him to find Gilgamesh and all the other warriors deep in slumber. He shouted at Gilgamesh, "Wake, mighty king! The sun has almost set, and still, you sleep! Wake now or the warriors' mothers will begin to mourn for their sons!"

Gilgamesh did not stir no matter how loud Enkidu yelled directly into his ear. Enkidu took a cloth soaked in oil and slapped it against Gilgamesh's chest. Finally, Gilgamesh woke with a start and jumped straight to his feet. He glared down at Enkidu, "What is wrong with me that I am sleeping like a babe in his mother's arms? Was that a god or a man who did this to me? I will not leave before I find out!"

Enkidu was becoming increasingly afraid of the whole situation. He tried to make his lord see reason. "You haven't even seen him! I have, and he is terrible to behold! His mouth is like a dragon's, and on his face, he wears the grimace of a lion. His chest holds the waters of a flood. No man dares go near him!" Enkidu decided he had had enough. "I am not going any further into the mountains. I know what waits there, and it is certain death. I will return to the city. I will tell your mother of your death and watch her weep!"

"Enkidu, if we work together we cannot be beaten! Can you alone cut through a triple layer of cloth? Can you wash a man away with his back to the wall by yourself? Nay! But we could together! Together we can face anything," Gilgamesh told his servant.

"You don't know what you're up against," Enkidu cried, doggedly trying to make Gilgamesh see reason. "Let us turn back and go home, please!"

"I don't care what you say; we are going! Come on!" Gilgamesh strode off into the forest, leaving Enkidu to scramble miserably after him.

Humbaba was waiting for them in his house. The demon's gaze meant certain death, and he proclaimed guilt with the shake of his head. As Gilgamesh got closer, he found himself suffused with terror. His foot stuck to the ground by the big toe. He could go no further.

Humbaba called out, "Hello! Welcome! You are a mighty sapling grown into a tree. You, who the gods favor, the mighty bull, standing angrily on the ground. Your mother knew how to make a fine son, and your nurse knew how to raise you well! Be not afraid. Place your hand on the ground and be at your ease."

Gilgamesh relaxed and put his hand on the ground. "Oh, mighty Humbaba, whose forest is not known, I swear by the life of my parents, I have come to offer you my sister, Enmebaragesi, in marriage. I will also give you another sister, Peshtur, to be your mistress and warm your bed. I want to be your kinsman! Just give me one of your auras so we can be close!"

Humbaba thought this was a very good offer and gave up one of his auras. Enkidu and the warriors cut a cedar to seal the deal. Crafty Gilgamesh was not done yet. The second gift is unknown, but Humbaba does give Gilgamesh another one of his auras.

The third aura was given in exchange for flour of the highest quality and the purest water to be found. Gilgamesh continued to sweet talk Humbaba into giving up his auras. He promised him sandals for his big feet and sandals for his little feet, too. Precious gems and stones were promised for his sixth aura, and all the while, Gilgamesh crept closer and closer to Humbaba as he released his auras. Finally, Humbaba gave up his seventh and final aura and was without any protection.

Gilgamesh slipped up next to Humbaba and made like he was about to kiss him like a brother but hit him in the face with his fist instead. Humbaba, caught by surprise and without the protection of his auras, was stunned. He growled and bared his teeth as Gilgamesh and Enkidu tied him up with ropes. The dragged him outside where they made him sit on the ground. Humbaba sat and wept bitterly.

He cried, "Oh, Shamash! I had no mother and no father. I am a child of the mountain. Gilgamesh has tricked me even though he swore by the mountain, the heavens, and the underworld!"

Gilgamesh looked at the demon weeping in the dirt at his feet. His heart was softened toward him. He said to Enkidu, "We should let him go back to his mother. Like releasing a bird, let him go back to his mountain."

Enkidu answered him saying, "You may be a well-raised, mighty king, but you know nothing. You will end up in Namtar's embrace if you are not careful! If you let this bird go back to the mountain, you will never return home!"

Humbaba sneered at Enkidu. "You are a servant. Why do you speak such words to your lord? You shouldn't speak such words to your master!"

Enkidu flew into a rage at Humbaba's words and cut off his head. He and Gilgamesh put the demon's head in a bag and took it to the gods. They knelt before Enlil and kissed the ground before him. Gilgamesh opened the bag and set the severed head at Enlil's feet.

Enlil frowned down at the offering. He spoke to Gilgamesh and Enkidu in anger. "Why have you done this? Who laid down the command that Humbaba was to be taken from this earth? You should have broken bread with him and treated him well! It was not your place to take his life!"

Enlil was saddened by the loss of Humbaba and used his powers to settle the auras that had been scattered with the demon's death. The first aura was sent to the field, the second to the river, and the third to the canebrake. The fourth aura was distributed to the lion, and the fifth went to the woods. The sixth aura was sent to the palace, and Enlil gave the seventh aura to Nungal, a goddess of the Underworld.

There is a second version of this poem, but it is largely similar to this version. The main difference is that instead of Gilgamesh awakening from the deep sleep, Humbaba set on them, attacking while everyone slept except Enkidu. Enkidu surges forward to meet the demon, but he worries that he is not brave enough. The fighting wakes Gilgamesh and the others. Gilgamesh seeks intervention from Ea, asking that Ea guides his words so he can trick Humbaba. Enkidu is the conduit for the words from the god and tells Gilgamesh what to say. They trick Humbaba, and the rest of the story is the same.

# The Envoys of Akka

This is another Sumerian poem that is independent of the epic. It is the most well preserved of all the poems. While short, it gives the history of how Gilgamesh became the Lord of Kish as well as Uruk. King Akka and his forces have laid siege on Uruk and have sent a messenger in with terms of surrender.

Gilgamesh received the emissary from Kish and heard the demands from their great leader, Akka. He took the matter to the Elders of Uruk. "They will make us slaves. We will do their drudgery! Let us rise up and fight for our independence," Gilgamesh urged.

The Elders did not agree. They flatly responded that they did not support war with Kish. Gilgamesh heard their counsel and then, completely disregarded it.

Gilgamesh gathered his soldiers and the young men of the city around him. "The army of Kish threatens our walls. They will make slaves of us. We will carry water and dig their wells. I think we should go to war to fight for our independence!"

The young men of the city considered this. Ultimately, they decided that submitting to Akka's demands would be very much like holding a donkey's tail – unpredictable at best and painful at worst. "Our city of Uruk is the smithy of the gods, blessed and beloved with the great temple of Ishtar. You are their prince and our mighty king! We are not afraid of that army; it is but a rabble! Let us stand up and fight for our city and our freedom!"

Buoyed by the young men's reaction, Gilgamesh ordered Enkidu to make preparations to go to war. "Make yourselves terrifying and bold," he told Enkidu. "When the enemy arrives at our gate, we want him confused and afraid."

Despite the brave words, after more than ten days of siege by Akka and his forces, the men of Uruk were beginning to panic and weaken. Gilgamesh rallied them and asked for a volunteer to go as an envoy to Akka. One of his loyal servants, Birhurturra, volunteered for the duty.

As soon as Birhurturra crossed beyond enemy lines, he was beaten before he was taken to the ruler of Kish, Akka. He addressed Akka, attempting to give him Gilgamesh's message. However, while he was speaking, Akka noticed a man walking on the wall of Uruk and interrupted Birhurturra.

"Who is that man on the wall? Is that your king?"

Birhurturra saw that it was the steward of Uruk and not Gilgamesh. He answered Akka, "No, that is not my king. If it were my king with his fearsome countenance, beard of lapis, and fingers of fire, wouldn't your men be cowering and trembling where they stand? Wouldn't Akka, the great ruler of Kish, be his prisoner in the heart of Uruk?"

Birhurturra paid dearly for his words of defiance. They beat him again, leaving no part of him unbruised. Another man stood on the wall. This time, it was Gilgamesh, and he was terrible to behold. As he stood on the wall, looking down over the enemy's army with anger in his eyes, Enkidu led the warriors of Uruk out of the city's gate.

Akka asked Birhurturra again, "Who is the man on the wall? Is that your king?"

Birhurturra stood as straight as he was able despite his injuries and proclaimed proudly, "Yes, that is my king. Gilgamesh is coming, and it will be as I said it would be!"

And so, it was. The army of Kish trembled and cowered. They were beaten back and cut down by the forces of Uruk. Akka fell prisoner and was soon held prisoner by Gilgamesh in the heart of Uruk.

Gilgamesh spoke to Akka, "Oh great Akka, once you sheltered me. You gave me back my life when I thought it was lost."

Akka nodded, remembering the incident. "I did indeed, mighty Gilgamesh, King of Uruk. I am now the one in need. Repay me the favor I once granted you!"

Gilgamesh honored his debt and let Akka go free. However, the city of Kish became a sovereign state of Uruk and from then on, was under Gilgamesh's rule.

## The Bull of Heaven

This rendition of the story of Gilgamesh and the Bull of Heaven is quite different than the standard version included in the epic, though the outcome is the same. Fewer copies exist of this poem than the standard version. Some of the translation is a bit of an educated guess based on knowledge of the story. There is the supposition that this poem was written as a political allegory of the struggles of Sumer under the rule of the Akkade. However, others claim that it could simply be a story told to entertain and amuse.

The poem begins with a hymn about he mighty and wonderful King Gilgamesh before transitioning into a conversation with his mother, Ninsun. The text is badly damaged in this part, but it appears that Ninsun is encouraging her son to see about his kingly duties. Gilgamesh leaves her to go to Uruk to take care of things. As he enters the gates of Uruk, he is accosted by Ishtar, the goddess of love and sexuality.

"Oh, mighty Gilgamesh, I would have you. You, the Wild Bull, shall be mine. I will not let you leave until I am done with you. I will not let you go to my temple and do your kingly duty of judgment until I am sated."

Unable to proceed into the city, Gilgamesh turned and went back to his mother to seek her counsel. When he told her of Ishtar's proposition (which interestingly took place at the city gate where it was customary for prostitutes to ply their trade), Ninsun told her son that he must not accept her advances for she would weaken Gilgamesh.

Gilgamesh returned to the city and confronted Ishtar. "My Lady Ishtar, you must not interfere with my duties as King! You must allow me to pass into my city. I will fill your pens with wild bulls and sheep if you let me pass!"

There is a large section missing from the poem, but it is assumed that Ishtar did not give in gracefully. If the poem follows the standard version, after Ishtar's continued refusal to allow Gilgamesh to pass, he ridiculed her and recited the fates of her past lovers. The poem resumes with Ishtar in her father's palace in the Heavens.

Ishtar wept bitterly, sobbing over her rejection. Her father, Anu, found her and asked, "My beloved daughter, why do you weep?"

"The Wild Bull of Uruk has refused me. He is on a rampage in the city and will not let me give myself to him. He has turned me away!" Ishtar cried on her father's shoulder, and when she regained some of her composure, there was fury in her heart. "Please, Father, give me the Bull of Heaven. Let me set it loose on Gilgamesh and make him pay for his insult to me!"

Anu shook his head. "The Bull of Heaven would have nothing to eat or drink on the Earth. He is a creature of the skies and must remain there."

Ishtar would not accept this. "If you do not give me the Bull of Heaven, I shall scream and scream until the world is covered in despair and darkness."

Anu, who knew the power of his daughter's terrifying scream, had no choice. He gave her the Bull of Heaven.

Ishtar led the Great Bull out of the sky and unleashed it on Earth. The bull drank the rivers dry and ate all of the grass and even an enormous date grove. Lugalgabangal, the royal minstrel, saw the devastation and hurried to tell his liege.

"Oh, my king, while you sit and eat and drink in your palace, the Great Bull of Heaven is laying waste to your country. It has eaten the grass and drained the rivers. The mighty date grove is gone! You must make haste and save your country!"

Gilgamesh was not to be hurried, however. He finished his feast, and once he was full of food and wine, he set about making preparations to battle the Bull of Heaven. He strapped on his battle gear and sent his sisters to make offerings to the gods. He spoke to his mother before leaving.

"I am going to smite the Bull of Heaven. His meat will be given to the poor of the city, and his hide will be sent to the tanners to cloth the people. I will send his giant horns to Ishtar's temple that she may drink from them." With the confidence of a king, Gilgamesh went to face the Bull of Heaven, with Enkidu at his side.

Gilgamesh taunted the Bull, telling him that he would feed his meat to his people and his hide would be worn on their backs. Enkidu circled behind the bull and grabbed him by the tail. Enkidu cried out to his king, "Oh mighty Gilgamesh, who was born and raised well, who is a sapling grown to strength, strike now and strike true!"

Gilgamesh swung his battle ax and cleaved the head bull's head from his body. The body crumpled to the earth, like a big lump of clay. Ishtar had watched the whole thing from the wall of the city. Gilgamesh was furious with her. He cut off the hind leg of the beast and hurled it at her. She turned into a dove and flew to the heavens. The leg knocked down a large section of the city's wall.

Gilgamesh did as he said he would and distributed the meat and the hide among his people.

Gilgamesh is the most well-known of all Mesopotamian kings and myths. His legendary adventures served as the foundation for many tales throughout literary history. It isn't difficult to find parallels between him and Odysseus. However, Gilgamesh is far from the only tale worth telling from ancient Mesopotamia!

# Chapter 4 The Descent of Ishtar

Ishtar was one of the most popular of all Mesopotamian deities. She was the patron god of Uruk and has more stories and myths written about her than any other god. As the goddess of love and war, she has polar sides to her personality. Her brother, Shamash, the sun god, hinted to her that it was high time she married. She was beautiful and impetuous, and no shortage of men and gods would be willing to marry her.

Shamash turned her eyes toward the shepherd, Dumuzid. Ishtar turned up her nose at the suggestion. She told her brother, "I will not be the wife of a shepherd! I am a goddess; I am a star! I will most certainly not wed a lowly shepherd!"

Shamash was not so easily deterred. "Come, Sister. The shepherd is the finest in the land. His milk is sweet, and his butter is perfect. Everything he touches is good. He will be a good husband to you, Ishtar. He will give you jewels and love you well. Why do you resist?"

Ishtar shook her head stubbornly. "His soft garments of wool will not sway me. I will marry the farmer with his fields of grain and plenty. I will not marry the shepherd!"

Dumuzid walked beside Ishtar and asked her, "Why do you prefer the farmer to me? If he offers you a robe of fine black wool, it is because he got it from my fine black sheep. If he offers you fine wool of white, it is because he got the wool from my best white sheep. His brewed beer is sweet, but not as sweet as my milk or butter. His mead is smooth but not as smooth as my whipped milk. The farmer is a good man, but he cannot offer you what I can."

Ishtar considered the shepherd's words, and her heart warmed toward him.

Dumuzid left Ishtar feeling elated and knowing with Shamash on his side, Ishtar would be his wife. As he let his sheep graze on the banks of the river, the farmer, Enkimdu, approached. Dumuzid met him and challenged him for the lady's hand.

Enkimdu did not accept the challenge. "Why would I fight with you, Shepherd? You have done nothing to cross me. Let your sheep graze along my rivers and graze on the stubble of my fields. I do not contest your claim to the Lady Ishtar."

This cheered Dumuzid further, and he promised the farmer that they would always be friends. The farmer accepted this and said that he would bring bags of grain and beans to honor the married couple.

Thus, Ishtar and Dumuzid were wed. While she may have been initially reluctant to marry him, Ishtar fell head over heels in love with Dumuzid. Their wedding night was recorded in vivid, erotic detail that clearly illustrated their passionate connection.

However, it was not in Ishtar's nature to be monogamous or to stay at home and play the happy homemaker. She was often restless and was very active in and around the city of Uruk. After the slaying of the Bull of Heaven in the *Epic of Gilgamesh*, Ishtar found herself growing restless in her heavenly court.

Some accounts show that Ishtar was visited by two small demons. They whispered to her about how much power her sister, Ereshkigal, Queen of the Underworld, possessed. They tempted her with the notion that Ishtar's powers would know no rival if she claimed both the throne of Heaven and the throne of Irkalla. Before they left, the demons of mischief whispered counsel of how to act in the Underworld. They reminded her, above all else, not to dress in royal finery.

After the demon's visit, Ishtar sat in the heavens, but her thoughts turned to the Underworld. She tried to think of other things, but her mind refused to leave the world below. Eventually, she decided that she needed to travel to the

Underworld. She left her seat in the heavens and her temples on the Earth to descend into the Underworld.

Ishtar made her preparations for the journey. She gathered first the divine providences of civilization, the Me, and held them close about her. She arranged her hair and donned a turban that was fit for traveling. Ishtar decorated her eyes with oil and murmured, "Come, oh men, to me!" Her body she draped in royal finery and beads of lapis hung around her neck. She strapped on her breastplate and golden bracelets. Finally, she took up her measuring rod and line of lapis and set out on her journey.

Her servant, Ninshubur, traveled with her. Ishtar said to her, "Ninshubur, my faithful companion, your counsel is always sound, and you have stood bravely by my side. I am bound for the Underworld. Hear my words and follow my instructions! If I do not return, you must start the lament for me and beat the drum throughout the assembly of gods. You must wail and tear at your hair and eyes. Dress like a beggar and mourn me!

"Then, go to the holy temple of Enlil in Nippur. Fall on your knees and call to him 'Oh, mighty Enlil! Your daughter is trapped in the Underworld! Do not leave her there! Do not let your bright silver tarnish or your lapis be broken for stonework! Do not forsake the high priestess to the darkness of the Underworld!'

"If Enlil will not stir himself to come to my aid, seek out Sin, god of the moon, and give him the same message. If Sin will not help, go to Ea, the mighty god of the sea. Seek him in his temple Eridug and tell him my tale of woe. He holds creation and the waters of life. He above all others can rescue me!"

They traveled onward. As they neared the Underworld, Ishtar bade her servant leave her and reminded Ninshubur not to forget her instruction.

When Ishtar arrived at the gate to the Underworld, she pushed hard against it and found it barred to her. She pounded on the door and shouted, "Neti, Gate Keeper of the Darkness, open the door!"

Neti calmly answered back, "Who are you? Who pounds on my door?"

Ishtar proclaimed in response, "I am the Queen of Heaven! I am traveling to the East and demand passage!"

Neti again replied with a tranquil calm, "If you are Ishtar, tell me why the Queen of Heaven would want to pass through the lands from which none return?"

Ishtar, with growing impatience, shouted through the gate, "I have come to see my sister, Ereshkigal, Queen of the Dead. The Great Bull of Heaven, her husband, Gugalanna, has been slain! I am here for the funeral! Let us pour beer in the cup and have done with it!"

"I will take your message to my Queen. You will wait here," Neti answered in the same unhurried tone and left to tell his Queen of her visitor.

Neti found Queen Ereshkigal and bowed low before her. "My Queen! There is a maid at the gate. She is beautiful beyond knowing. She is the width and breadth of heaven and earth. She is stronger than a foundation of stone. She is requesting passage. She has with her the divine principles of civilization and wears jewels and a breastplate. Her robes are finely made, and she carries a measuring rod and line of lapis."

Queen Ereshkigal knew that her sister Ishtar was waiting at her gate, and she was not happy. Her husband, the Great Bull of Heaven, was dead because of Ishtar's temper tantrum after being spurned by the mighty King Gilgamesh. Ereshkigal slapped her leg and bit her lip in frustration. She thought about what to do and finally came to a decision. She said to Neti, "Go tell Ishtar that she may cross my domain. Before she enters, bar each of the seven gates. Open each one a crack but only after she has shed some of her royal finery! Let my sister enter my presence humbled and bowed low!"

Neti hastened back to the gate, barring each of the seven gates as he went. To Ishtar, he said, "Come and enter, Queen Ishtar." As she passed through the gates, Neti removed her turban.

Ishtar was outraged. "What is this? What are you doing taking my headdress," she cried, angrily.

Neti, unflappable as ever, replied, "Be quiet, Ishtar. These are the ways of the Underworld. They are perfect and above question." He led her to the next gate. Again, he opened it a crack, and as Ishtar stepped through, her small necklace of lapis was removed.

"How dare you take my things! This is outrageous," Ishtar seethed.

Neti merely shrugged and answered as before. "Be quiet, Ishtar. These are the ways of the Underworld. They are perfect and above question."

And so, it went through each gate. At the third gate, Ishtar lost the large jewels from her breastplate, and at the fourth, her breastplate was taken. At the fifth gate, Neti claimed her bracelet of gold. The sixth gate cost Ishtar her measuring rod and line made of lapis. Finally, at the seventh gate, Ishtar was forced to give up her royal robes.

Naked and humbled, Ishtar went in front of her sister and bowed. Ereshkigal rose from her throne and looked down on her sister. Ishtar went to her as if into a sisterly embrace. The Annuna surrounded them and as the judges of the Underworld, passed judgment on Ishtar.

As Ishtar reached her sister, Ereshkigal, the Queen of the Darkness, fixed her with her gaze of death. With a wrathful cry of anguish that proclaimed Ishtar's doom, Ereshkigal struck Ishtar down dead.

Her corpse turned to rotting meat, and the vengeful Queen of the Underworld hung it from a hook on the wall for all to see.

Ninshubur, Ishtar's faithful servant, followed her mistress's orders and after three days, she began her lament for her fallen mistress. She beat the drum through temples of the gods and dressed in a sack to show her mourning. She tore at her hair and eyes and made her way to Ekur.

In the house of Enlil, Ninshubur threw herself prostrate before Enlil. She begged, "Please, Mighty Father Enlil, do not let your daughter be kept in the Underworld! Do not forget Ishtar and let her be like silver that tarnishes. Do not let her be like precious lapis broken for the work of the stone mason. Do not let my Lady Ishtar be killed!"

Enlil looked down at Ninshubur and shook his head. "My daughter Ishtar is power hungry. She wants the power of the heavens and the power of the darkness. She knew what would happen if she went to the Underworld. Everyone knows that if you go there, you do not return!" With that condemnation, Enlil turned away from the kneeling servant.

Ninshubur remembered her lady's instructions and went next to Urim to seek the house of the god Sin. She bowed and pleaded with the god of the moon, reciting her message.

Sin was no more sympathetic than Enlil. "My daughter Ishtar is greedy! She has the powers of the heavens, and yet, she wants more. She holds the seven divine powers of civilization but still, she hungers! The powers of the Underworld should not be sought! She knew the rules and knew that no one ever returns from there. Her punishment is just!" Sin turned his back on Ninshubur and would not yield.

Undeterred, Ninshubur went to Eridug. In the house of Ea, she knelt before the wisest of the gods and recited what she had been told to say.

Ea's face softened in concern. "Oh, Ishtar, my beautiful daughter. What have you done? I am worried about you!" Ea knew that Ishtar was dead in the Underworld, for only the dead are allowed within its walls. So, he scraped dirt from under one fingernail and created a *galla*, a person of no specific gender, and gave it the plant of life. He created another *galla* from the dirt under another nail and gave it the water of life. He dispatched his creations to the underworld to rescue Ishtar. Before they left, he told the creatures, "Go now to the Kingdom of Darkness. Go to the Underworld and slip in like phantoms. Be like flies and go unnoticed. Find Ereshkigal, Queen of the Underworld. She will be easy to find. Her shoulders will be uncovered, and her breasts will be bare. Her hair is a riot around her head like a stew of leeks. The pains of labor are heavy upon her.

"Go to her and be sympathetic to her pain and distress. When she cries out about her heart and her liver, speak gently to her and tell her you understand. She will bid you welcome, for she is rarely dealt with gently. When she offers you a favor in return for your kindness, make her swear by heaven and earth that she will honor that favor.

"She will offer you a river of water and a field full of grain. Do not accept these gifts. When she asks you what you want, tell her that you want the corpse hanging on the wall. She will tell you that it is the body of your queen. Reply that it does not matter if it is your queen or your king, you want the body on the wall. She will give it to you, for she cannot refuse her promised favor.

"Take the body and sprinkle the plant and water of life over it. Ishtar shall rise from the dead!"

The galla went to the Underworld and followed Ea's instructions. They spoke kindly to the Queen of the Dead, and she, in turn, promised a favor. They resisted her tempting offers and demanded the body of Ishtar as their favor. Once they had the goddess's lifeless body, they sprinkled it with the plant and water of life. Ishtar rose from the dead.

The galla tried to leave with Ishtar in tow, but Ereshkigal forbade it. "You may have brought my sister, Ishtar, back to life, but she cannot leave here! No one who enters here may leave!"

The Annuna, the wise and powerful judges of the dead, demanded, "If Ishtar leaves this place, she must bring us one to take her place!"

Ishtar agreed to this and was allowed to return to the land of the living. However, four demons accompanied her. The demons knew not hunger or thirst. They knew not pleasure or pain. They could not be bribed or corrupted in any manner. They would see Ishtar's grisly deed done.

At the gate of the Underworld, Ninshubur waited. She sat in the dust and was dressed in a sack. Her face was stained with tears for her mistress. She was there when the gate opened and Ishtar, with her unholy companions, passed through.

The demons saw Ninshubur there and said to Ishtar, "We will take her in exchange for you. Go now, Lady, to your city." The demons made to grab Ninshubur, but Ishtar stopped them.

"This is my most trusted servant and loyal friend! She heeded my words and followed my instructions. She spoke to the great gods Enlil, Sin, and Ea for me. I owe my life to her! You cannot have her! Come with me to Umma!"

So, Ishtar, Ninshubur, and the demon guards went to the city of Umma. There Ishtar found Cara, her son as well as minstrel and hairdresser. The demons felt he would be a good substitution for Ishtar in the Underworld.

Cara had thrown himself at Ishtar's feet when he saw his mistress. His face was covered in grime, and he wore a sack. His mourning was evident. "You cannot have Cara! I cannot live without him! Let us go on to Bad-tibira."

They trooped to Bad-tibira. There they found Ishtar's youngest son, Lulal. He, too, was sitting in the dirt, wearing only a sack in mourning of his mother's fate. The demons once again attempted to take their hostage, but Ishtar blocked them, for Lulal had been a faithful son and mourned his mother properly. Ishtar declared they would walk on to Kulaba, where the great green apple tree grew.

The little party marched onward until in the orchard they came across Dumuzid, Ishtar's husband. He was dressed in his royal robes and finery. He sat on a magnificent throne and had obviously not been mourning his wife.

Dumuzid's face drained of all color. He had just had a dream that foretold tragedy for him, and now it seemed like it was coming true. He had woken that morning in a terrible state. His dream had been so vivid it was not until he was running across the field screaming that he realized he was not dead. He had gone straight to his sister, so she could tell him what his dream meant.

"Oh, my dear Geshtinanna, my dear sister, listen now to the torment of my night! The reeds were rising all around me. They just kept getting bigger and bigger. One shook its head at me, and another went away from me. I could not grasp it. The forest loomed over me, growing ever greater. My brazier was extinguished. My churns were overturned and empty. My cup was not on its peg on the wall and lay discarded and empty. My shepherd's staff was gone from me as well. As I watched, an owl-demon stole a lamb from the pen. A falcon carried off a sparrow from its perch on the reed fence. The billy-goats dug their beards through the dirt, and my mighty rams churned up the ground beneath their hooves. I was no longer. I was dead, and my herd was being haunted!"

Geshtinanna had heard his words and urged him not to share his dream with anyone else. "This is not a fortuitous dream, brother! The reeds growing around you are your enemies lying in wait to ambush you. The single reed that shook its head is our mother, and the reed being separated from you is me, your dear sister. The looming forest symbolizes an evil man coming for you. Your overturned churns show that he will take the sheep herd for his own. Your cup missing from the peg is you falling from our mother's lap. Your staff is missing because the demons have set fire to it. The owl-demon and falcon and the sparrow mean the evil man will enter and destroy your sheep house. The goats with their beards in the dirt and the rams churning up the earth beneath their feet show my grief will be great at your loss. Oh, Dumuzid, this is terrible!"

His sister's words echoed in his head when he saw Ishtar approach with her demons. On the wind, he heard his sister's cries, too late, warning him that his enemies approached.

The demons were quite restless and wanted to return to the Underworld. They fell upon Dumuzid and surrounded him. Ishtar made no move to stop them. They emptied Dumuzid's milk churns, and they refused to let him play his flute or beg for his life.

Ishtar looked at her husband coldly, and in her eyes, he saw his death. "What is taking so long? Take him to the Underworld and see that my debt is paid!"

The demons began to haul Dumuzid away. He cried out to the heavens to his brother-in-law, Shamash. "Oh, great Shamash, hear my plea! Remember, I brought your mother butter, and we are related! Do not forsake me now! Turn me into a snake so I might escape these demons!"

Shamash heard Dumuzid's cries and was moved by his tears. He granted Dumuzid's wish and transformed him into a snake. With his new slithery form, Dumuzid slipped from the demon's grasp and escaped.

Ishtar tore at her hair in great distress. She cried in anguish. No one could find Dumuzid. Time passed, and the demons of the Underworld searched and searched for the shepherd turned serpent. The demons did not know fatigue, hunger, or thirst. They searched relentlessly.

One day, they caught Dumuzid's sister, Geshtinanna, in the sheep pen, where she was doing her best to tend to her brother's flock. They offered her all of the water in the river if she would tell them where Dumuzid hid. She refused. She refused their offer of the finest food in all the land. She withstood their torture and never revealed her brother's secret.

Dumuzid had told his location to only one other person, his best friend, whose name we do not know. The demons found this friend and questioned him. When they offered their bribes of food and water, the friend accepted. He told them they could find Dumuzid in the canals of Arali. The demons flew to the canals and there as promised, they found poor Dumuzid.

He wept bitter tears and cried, "My sister gave me life, and my friend gave me death! If anyone should come across a sister abandoned in the street, lift her up and kiss her. But if anyone should come by a friend abandoned in the street, pass him by and let him rot!"

The demons bound Dumuzid's hands and began to haul him off to the Underworld. Dumuzid cried out to Shamash, who had shown favor to him before. "Shamash, oh Great Sun God! I brought the wedding gifts to Unug. I kiss the lips of the holy Ishtar. Change me into a gazelle that I might live!"

Shamash heard Dumuzid's pleas. He always had liked Dumuzid and didn't want to see him lost to the Underworld forever. So, he granted the request and changed Dumuzid into a gazelle. The bonds on his wrists slipped impotently off his gazelle legs as he bounded away from the demon's clutches.

The demons did not give up their chase. They, who were not born of parents and had no siblings, could not conceive of family loyalty. However, they finally decided after nearly catching Dumuzid several times, only to have Shamash turn him into something so he could escape, that they should watch Geshtinanna. They figured he would eventually come back to his sister and his sheep.

Their hunch paid off. As the demons watched, they saw a new sheep in the flock and knew that Dumuzid had returned. They waited until the flock was unsupervised and struck quickly and with mercy. They turned over the churns and tore down the cup from the peg. They set fire to Dumuzid's staff and stole away with one of the lambs. There was chaos all around, and when it settled, Dumuzid lay dead in the center of his sheep pen.

With their trophy, the demons retreated to Irkalla, the balance of life and death once again restored.

Geshtinanna was distraught, and she sang a lament for her brother. Ishtar and her mother joined Geshtinanna in her grief. Ishtar told her how sorry she was that Dumuzid was gone. Even though Dumuzid hadn't grieved her passing, she was devastated by his.

The women grieved and lamented until a fly alighted on Ishtar's shoulder and whispered, "I can show you where your husband is, but what will you do for me if I do?"

Ishtar promised the fly that the beer house's ale jugs would overflow just for it. The fly told them where to go. The women found Dumuzid's shade and were bitterly sad. Not only were they heartbroken, the flocks were not doing well, and the earth was not fertile without Dumuzid. Ishtar decreed that to ease Dumuzid's suffering and bring fertility to the Earth and vitality to herds, Dumuzid would only spend half the year in the Underworld. His sister, the ever faithful Geshtinanna, would take his place for the other half of the year.

The flocks prospered, and the Earth was fertile while Dumuzid walked the fields protecting his flocks. When he descended to the Underworld, he took with him the greenness from the fields and the fatness from the sheep. And thus, summer and winter were established in Mesopotamia.

# Chapter 5 Enki and Inanna

This short story details a meeting between the god of wisdom and the Queen of Heaven. The concept of the Me, or the divine knowledge and guiding principles of civilization, is a recurrent one throughout Mesopotamian literature. Sometimes compiled as the Tablet of Destinies, the Me represent great power and change hands among the gods several times. This swapping around of the most precious knowledge known to the gods was probably a result of shifts of cult followings and worshippers. Whoever was the god with the largest following at the time, the myth was created so they would control the Me.

*Note: Enki and Ea are the same deities, god of the sea. Ishtar and Inanna are the same deities as well, Queen of Heaven and goddess of love, sexuality, and beauty. We use Enki and Inanna here to stay true to the original text of the myth.*

Inanna, Queen of Heaven, decided that she was ready to embrace her power as queen. Up to this point, she had not fully explored her powers as the goddess of love and sexuality. However, as she looked at herself in the mirror and combed out her beautiful hair, she knew it was time to show the other gods she was a force to be reckoned with. So, she donned her crown and dressed in her finest raiment. With a determined step, she traveled to the court of Enki at his temple of Eridug.

Enki, who had the power of foresight, saw that his daughter, Inanna, was heading his way. He called his advisor, Isimud, who hurried to his master's side. "Isimud, the Lady Inanna approaches. When she arrives, make her feel welcome. Feed her the best butter cakes and pour her clear, sweet water. Offer her beer in the shade of the Lion's Gate. Fuss over her and make her feel like she is as great as Anu!"

Isimud assured his master that he would take care of everything and set off to make his preparations. When Inanna arrived, he did exactly as he had been instructed to do. Inanna was impressed with her reception and was delighted when Enki joined her.

They sat together, and the beer flowed freely. They sampled Enki's best wine and were having a high time. Then, the drinking competition began. The mugs of beer overflowed as Enki and Inanna sought to drink each other under the table.

As they got progressively drunker, Enki was moving faster toward inebriation than Inanna and starting to feel magnanimous. He boasted about how much he cared about Inanna and how he wanted to give her something. His clear-headed wisdom had deserted him with the drink, so he thought he would offer her the Me of heroism. He raised his voice and proclaimed, "I, Enki, Master of the Apsu, with my power, I give my daughter, Inanna, Holy Queen of Heaven, the Me of heroism!"

Inanna slapped her hand on the table and cried, "I shall have it!"

Enki, sinking ever deeper in his cups, was pleased by Inanna's reaction. He gave her the Me of righteousness, strife, kindness, and respect. After each of them, Inanna slapped the table and claimed it. On and on her father went, giving her more and more of the precious principles that gave him power and guided civilization. He gave her deceit, rejoicing, awe, and reverent silence. He gave her the crafts of the scribe, smith, leatherworker, builder, and reed-worker. Inanna, who was sobering quickly, pounced on each one. Finally, he passed on all the Me, even the holy rites, wisdom, judging, and triumph.

Inanna gathered up all the Me and held them close about her. She plied Enki with more and more beer until he slipped into a drunken stupor. Then, Inanna left her father's court as quickly as she could. She knew Enki would think better of his generosity once he had sobered up. She wanted to be beyond his reach before that happened.

Enki, who was undoubtedly feeling pretty rough the next day, called for his advisor, Isimud once the alcohol had cleared from his head. "What has happened? Where are the Me? Where is my daughter?"

Isimud answered, "My Lord, my sweet master! You gave the Me to Inanna! You gave them all to her, and she claimed each one!"

Enki's heart sank. He knew his daughter wasn't likely to give them back out of the goodness of her heart. "Where is she? Has she gone past the city of Utu? Can I still reach her?"

Isimud shook his head sadly. "I'm sorry, my Lord, but she has left with the Boat of Heaven (which is not only a boat but contains the stolen Me)."

Enki sent his servant to intercept his daughter. "Go after her and take the demons. Seize the boat and bring it back to me!"

Isimud dutifully set off post-haste and caught up with Inanna at a quayside along her route. He called out to the Queen of Heaven, "My Lady Queen, please hear me! Your father has sent me with a message, and you must heed it! It is very serious!"

Inanna could very well guess what her father was going to say, but she replied, "Alright Isimud, I hear your words. What is this serious message from Enki?"

"He says that you may travel on to Uruk as you like, but you must give me the Boat of Heaven!"

Inanna's fury boiled over. "Has my father's word come to mean nothing? Is he a liar and a false god? Has he sent you here to go back on his words?"

While Inanna ranted about her father, Isimud signaled to the demons, and they set upon Inanna. Inanna cried out to her faithful servant, Ninshubur.

"Come and stand by my side. Your hands have never touched water. Your feet have never touched water. They cannot harm you!" Together, the women beat back the demons and fled in the Boat of Heaven.

Isimud returned to Enki and told him the bad news. Enki instructed him to gather fifty giants and go after Inanna again. The faithful servant did as he was told but had the same result. Again, he returned to his master empty-handed.

Enki sent him back out again and again. He sent water demons and all of the fish in the sea to try to claim the Boat of Heaven. When that didn't work, he tried the Guardians of Unug, and as a last-ditch effort, he tried to manipulate the waters of the canal into claiming the boat. Nothing worked, and Inanna reached her court in Uruk.

Her advisor and servant, Ninshubur, praised her lady, "My Lady Inanna! You have brought the sacred Me to Uruk! You have bested every trial sent to you! We shall enter the city in glory, and they shall know their queen!"

Inanna liked the sound of this, and as the Boat of Heaven made its way down the canals to her temple, the people poured into the streets to honor their queen.

Enki's faithful minister returned to his master for the last time and hung his head. He had failed, but Enki accepted the defeat. He watched as Inanna set about distributing the Me among her people. This pleased Enki because he saw that she didn't seek to use them herself. As she gave them to her people, the Me grew and multiplied. Inanna was showing her potential to be a very good queen. Pleased, Enki sent Isimud back one final time to Inanna. He reached her while her people celebrated her triumph. Isimud bowed low to Inanna and praised her name and bestowed her father's blessing.

This story probably represents the shifting of the power of the empire between Eridu and Uruk and Inanna's rise in popularity.

# Chapter 6 The Marriage of Nergal and Ereshkigal

Most people don't expect to find a passionate love story in the darkness of the Underworld. They also probably don't expect to see the touchy-feely side of the Queen of the Dead and the God of War and Pestilence. However, we have both of these unlikely events in *The Marriage of Nergal and Ereshkigal*.

There was to be a great banquet for all the gods. Anu was saddened because his daughter, Ereshkigal, Queen of the Underworld, would not be able to attend. He called his trusted messenger, Kakka, to him and bade him go to the Kingdom of Darkness with this message. Anu said, "I know, Daughter, that you are not able to come to my kingdom. Nor are we able to descend into yours. Send in your stead an emissary who can accept for you a gift from my table!"

Kakka heard the message and made the long journey from the heavens, down the long staircase, and down further yet to the gates of the Underworld. At the gate of the Underworld, he petitioned the gatekeeper, Neti, for entry. Neti led ever downward through the seven gates into the depths of darkness. Kakka was shown into a spacious courtyard where the Queen of the Dead waited. He bowed deeply to her before he stood and presented his father's message.

Ereshkigal's heart lightened at the message. She raised her voice in praise and gratitude. "Blessed be the mighty gods, Anu, Enlil, and Ea! Blessed be the Mother Goddess and Ninmah, Goddess of the Land!"

Kakka bowed again at the words spoken by Ereshkigal. "Indeed, Lady, peace is with Anu, Enlil, and Ea, the mightiest of all gods! Ninmah and the Mother Goddess thrive in peace as well! They send their blessing to you, Lady Queen, and hope that they find you well!"

Ereshkigal received the good wishes and eagerly accepted the invitation to send an emissary to her father's court for the banquet. She was not usually included in such things, and this gesture touched her deeply. "Come to me, Namtar," she called to her most trusted advisor. "Go to the banquet of my father in my stead. Stand there as I would and accept whatever he offers. Bring whatever he presents to you straight to me!"

Namtar swept a low bow and assured his queen he would see it done. He and Kakka made the long journey up through the seven gates of the Underworld, up the long staircase, and finally came to the heavens. Into the Assembly of Gods, the messengers went. When Namtar entered the hall, all of the great gods knelt before him out of deference for their sister. That is, all but one.

Nergal lounged in the back of the assembly and completely ignored the winks and hints from his fellow gods. He didn't understand what all the fuss was about. Ereshkigal had never done anything to inspire him to kneel before her emissary, and death was not anything he feared.

Ea, the wisest of gods, knew the trouble that Nergal had caused and attempted to distract Namtar from the insult. He called for food and wine, and Namtar was given the best wine before any of the rest of the gods were served. He was served the best food and given the choicest cuts of meats. The feast was legendary in its opulence, but Namtar did not forget about the god who did not kneel. He would tell his lady all about the insult when he returned to the Underworld.

Nergal was not particularly worried about Ereshkigal, but Ea urged him to prepare for a journey to the Underworld. He knew that Ereshkigal would not let the insult pass, and she would demand to know the name of the god who paid the insult. He also knew that if Ereshkigal and Nergal went to war, they would damage the barrier between the living and the dead. He couldn't let this happen. So, in an effort to appease Ereshkigal's ire, Ea instructed Nergal to build a throne.

The throne would be fashioned like the one that Shamash sat in as he traveled through the Underworld at night. Nergal followed the instructions of Ea. He cut mesu and tiaru trees and juniper added to them. Then, he harvested the kanaktu and simberru trees and wove them in amongst the others. Finally, he painted the chair according to the guidance of Ea.

Ea inspected the chair and approved it. The chair should allow Nergal to travel to and from the Land of the Dead. However, he had some last-minute advice for Nergal. He knew that if Nergal did even one small thing wrong, he would be trapped in the Underworld forever.

"Nergal, hear my words and heed them well! From the moment you enter the Underworld, you must not sit in any chair offered. You must not eat any bread or drink any mead they put in front of you. You must refuse their foot bath. Most of all, when Ereshkigal bathes and lets you see her body, you must not lay with her. You must not give in to the temptation to do the thing that men and women do!"

Nergal listened to Ea's advice and set out for the Underworld. When he reached the gate, he pounded on the door and demanded that Neti, the gatekeeper, let him in.

Neti replied, "I must check with my mistress before I let any pass." He went to his queen and told her of the strange god waiting at the gate.

Namtar volunteered to go to the gate and identify the visitor. When he got to the gate, fury rose in his chest. He knew this god. Going back to his mistress, he told her, "When I went to your father's court, the gods knelt before me in respect to you – all save one. Now he stands at your gate! Let me kill the traitor for the disrespect he showed you!"

Ereshkigal regarded her advisor and shook her head. "Namtar, you should not seek to wield more power than you have. You are not mighty Anu. Remember your place! Now, bring this god to me!"

Namtar bowed and went to fetch Nergal. He led him through each of the seven gates. They entered Ereshkigal's courtyard, and Nergal bowed low to her. He kissed the ground at her feet and then rose, saying, "Your father, Mighty Anu, sent me to sit on the throne of the dead and pass judgment on the great gods in Irkalla."

At Ereshkigal's command, her attendants brought a throne for Nergal. He refused to sit on it. They brought bread and mead, but again he refused.

Ereshkigal raised her eyebrows. "Surely, my Lord Nergal, you are tired and hungry after your journey. Take your ease. Do not spurn my hospitality. At least wash your feet!"

Nergal turned away the offered foot bath scented with sweet oils. Ereshkigal shrugged. "As you wish, Nergal. I am going to bathe."

Ereshkigal rose and went to the bath. She let him glimpse her body as she bathed and anointed herself with sweet oils. When she wrapped herself in her fine robe, she smiled an alluring smile at him. Nergal never stood a chance. His heart leaping in his chest, he went to her. With Ea's cautions completely forgotten, he embraced Ereshkigal and did with her what men and women do.

They lay in each other's embrace, The Queen of the Dead and the God of War, for six passion-filled days and six erotic nights.

On the seventh day, Nergal rose from his lover's bed. He kissed her and said, "I must go. Do not shake and tremble. I will come again to see you soon."

Ereshkigal's eyes flashed with fury, and her lips went white with anger. Nergal didn't stay around to talk any more about it. He went straight to the gate, sat upon the throne he had created, and proclaimed, "Your lady Ereshkigal sent me to take a message to her father, the great Anu. Open the gates and let me pass!"

The gates were opened, and Nergal rose from the Underworld. He went to the court of Anu, Enlil, and Ea. When they saw him, they said, "Nergal has come back to us! Ereshkigal's wrath will be terrible to behold! We must hide Nergal until her fury cools!"

Ea, the wise and powerful, sprinkled Nergal with magical waters and turned him into a cringing, bald man, who they hid amongst the rest of the Assembly of the Gods.

In the Underworld, Ereshkigal hadn't believed that Nergal would directly defy her by leaving the Underworld. She called to her handmaidens to prepare her bath and anoint the bedchamber.

Namtar told them not to bother and informed his mistress of Nergal's flight.

Ereshkigal wailed and fell from her throne, tears coursing down her face. She lay on the ground and wept. "Oh, Nergal! I had not had my fill of you! My delightful lover, I want more of you!"

Namtar hated to see his mistress so distressed. He urged her to send him to Anu and let him seize Nergal. "I will bring him back to you, my Lady Queen!"

Ereshkigal's wrath welled in her breast. Her fury overflowed, and in the terrible voice of death, she instructed Namtar to take her father a message. "Yes, Namtar," she said. "Go to my father's court. Tell my father, 'When I was a child, I did not play with other girls. I did not romp with other children. I was given to the dragon Kur and was sentenced to the darkness! You sent me a lover, and he has left me unclean and pregnant! You must send him back to me! I will know this happiness! If you do not, I will raise the dead and open the gates of Irkalla! The dead will cover the earth and decimate the living!'"

Namtar went straightaway to the court of Anu, Enlil, and Ea. They regarded the messenger in apparent confusion. "Namtar, emissary of my daughter, why are you here? What news do you bring?" asked Anu.

Namtar relayed the chilling message from Ereshkigal.

The mighty gods feigned surprise. Ea spoke to Namtar. "By all means, search the Assembly of Gods! If you see the god you seek, seize him and return him to your mistress!"

Namtar walked into the Assembly of Gods, and they all bowed before him. He regarded each god in turn but couldn't find Nergal amongst them. Disappointed, he went back to Ereshkigal with the news.

Namtar swept into a low bow and addressed his queen. "My Lady Ereshkigal, I went among the Assembly of Gods, but Nergal was not there. They all bowed before me, but there was one bald, cringing god who I did not recognize."

Ereshkigal was familiar with Ea's cunning and trickery. "Ea has sprinkled him with magical waters to disguise him. Seize the cringing, bald god and bring him to me!"

Namtar returned to the court of the mighty gods. Upon seeing the messenger, Anu asked him, "Why are you here Namtar?"

"I have come to seize the bald, cringing god. My Lady Ereshkigal commands it!"

Ea said to the emissary, "Search the Assembly. Seize the god you seek!"

Namtar entered the Assembly of Gods and sought the bald, cringing god. He looked at all of them, but the one he sought was not there.

From behind him, a voice came, "Namtar, Emissary of the Darkness, come now and eat and drink with us! Take your rest and wash your feet!"

Namtar turned and saw Nergal, who bowed and gave him all the deference he should have shown at their first meeting. Namtar accepted the gestures, and he let his anger at Nergal fade. As they shared bread and mead, Namtar told Nergal what he must do.

"Come again to Irkalla. Carry your sword and bow. Come in the throne you made and come prepared to take part in the hospitalities of the Underworld. Most importantly, you'll have to best each of the gatekeepers. Do not grapple with them or let them grasp you around the chest!"

Nergal listened to the counsel and carried out the preparations that Namtar had suggested. He crashed through the gates of the Underworld, one by one. He struck down Neti and all the other gatekeepers, never grappling with them.

The god of war strode straight into the Queen's courtyard. Ereshkigal sat proudly on her throne, wrapped in her fine linen. She stared coldly at Nergal. He laughed at her and with sudden ruthlessness, he seized the Queen by her hair and pulled her from her throne.

Ereshkigal cried out at the sudden attack but was overjoyed that her lover had returned. She was no wilting flower and gave as good as she got. They wrestled in the dirt, but their fury soon turned to passion. They ended up in bed and stayed there for another six days and nights.

On the morning of the seventh day, mighty Anu made his judgment heard. "Nergal, you are bound to the Underworld. You will reign next to Ereshkigal and be second only to her in the Kingdom of Darkness!"

And thus, Ereshkigal and Nergal were bound together, King and Queen of the Dead!

A later Assyrian version is much shorter and downplays the passionate love story. Nergal's nature as the god of war is a stronger theme.

This version parallels the Sumerian version about the banquet and Nergal's initial disrespect of Namtar. From there, the stories take two different tracks.

Following the banquet, Ea pulled Namtar off to the side. "I saw the god who did not kneel before you! I know your mistress will not stand for that and will demand he be punished. Go now into the Assembly of the Gods and find the one who insulted you. Take him with you to the Underworld!"

Namtar went one by one through all of the gods gathered in the Assembly. He did not see the one who had not knelt. One god crouched as if in terror, but he didn't look like the one who had not knelt, so Namtar passed him by.

Namtar returned the Underworld and told his liege all that had happened. Queen Ereshkigal said to Namtar, "I cannot allow this insult to pass. You will return to the court of my father in a month and see if you can find the god who dared defy me."

While Namtar was making the trip to the Underworld, Ea spoke to Nergal. "You must go to the Underworld. Ereshkigal will not let this insult stand, and she will find you. You are the god of war and must strike first!"

Nergal did not fear death, but he wasn't keen on the idea of marching down the Underworld to confront its queen on her home turf. "They will see me, and I will not be able to get past the gates."

Ea had a plan for that. "I will give you fourteen demons. They can bar the gates open for you."

So, Nergal and his band of demons went to the Underworld. Nergal pounded on the gates and bellowed, "Open the gates! I have been sent and would see your queen!"

Neti, the gatekeeper, summoned Namtar to inspect the stranger at the gates. He recognized Nergal as the god who had refused to kneel in the Assembly and went to his mistress. "My Lady Queen, the god who insulted you, who refused to kneel, he is at the gates!"

Ereshkigal didn't hesitate. "Bring him to me so I can show him what it means to fear death!"

Just as Namtar reached the gate to bid Nergal to enter, Nergal and his demons broke through the first gate. Nergal looked at Namtar, "You should be happy to see me! I know you've been waiting for this chance for a long time!" With that, he and his demons proceeded to barrel through each of the gates. He left demons to mind each gate, in case he needed to beat a hasty retreat. Scab, Lord of the Roof, Fits, Staggers, Expulsion, Bailiff, and Feverhot guarded the gates, keeping them open but letting none of the dead escape.

Nergal marched into the courtyard where Ereshkigal waited for him. She sat proudly on her throne and regarded him coldly as he approached. Nergal didn't pause for pleasantries. He pounced on Ereshkigal and pulled her from her throne by her hair. He cast her down into the dirt and drew his sword to deliver the killing blow.

"Wait! My Lord Nergal! Listen to my words! I have something to tell you!" Nergal stayed his sword and listened. "I give you kingship over the Earth. You can sit by my side and together we can rule! You shall be the Master of the Underworld, and I will be its Mistress!"

Nergal looked at the beautiful queen, and her tears moved his heart. He knelt beside her and kissed her. "My Queen, I shall be your king, and together we will reign supreme in the Kingdom of Irkalla." He raised her from the dirt and took her straight to bed.

# Chapter 7 The Myth of Adapa

Adapa's story is one of the most controversial of all of the ancient Mesopotamian myths that have been unearthed and translated. The tablets have only been found in two different spots, Egypt and the Royal Library of Ashurbanipal in Nineveh. The text was badly damaged, and the translation has been spotty, leading to the controversy. The tale told here is the most widely accepted version that has been compiled from all of the fragments.

Adapa was known as the greatest of the seven sages. He was the son of Ea, and Ea gave him all of the knowledge and the wisdom of the world. He did not, however, grant him eternal life. Adapa served the people of the ancient city of Eridu as a priest, advisor, and protector. He taught the people how to build their buildings and cities. He instructed them on law and numbers. He showed them how to grow crops and improve the health of their animals. Holy and pure, he presided over rituals and observed the rites of a priest. Adapa also helped the bakers make the bread, blessing it with his purity. He served the gods as well. He brought their bread and water offerings to the great temples in Eridu.

The last duty of Adapa's was fishing for the village. Every day he would go out past the reeds and marshes and onto the open sea to bring in the fish to feed the city. He set out in his sailboat one day, just like he had innumerable days before. The fishing was not going well, and he drifted across the still, mirrored surface of the sea.

Suddenly, a wind gusted, capsizing his boat. The South Wind swirled around him, intent on sending him down to dwell among the fishes. Adapa's anger flared, and he cursed the South Wind. "South Wind, I see you! You can toss me in the sea and send your fellows to blow me this way and that, but I will break your wing!"

At his words, the wings of the South Wind were broken, and it ceased to blow.

Seven days later, Anu noticed the stillness in the South. He called out to his advisor, Ilabrat. "Why is the South Wind not blowing? It has been still for many, many days now."

Ilabrat bowed to Anu and answered his liege. "My Lord, the South Wind's wings were broken by Adapa, son of Ea."

Anu's face clouded with thunder, and he pushed up from his throne. "He'd better have a good explanation for this! Bring him to me!"

Ea always kept track of what was going on in the heavens even though he dwelt deep in the waters of Apsu. He heard his brother's demand and sought out his favorite son. "Adapa, hear my words," he said earnestly. "You will soon be called to attend Anu in heaven. Heed my advice, and you might return here alive. Go to the heavens when you are called. Wear the raiment of mourning and let your hair be disheveled. As you approach Anu's court, you will meet two gatekeepers, Dumuzid and Gishzida. They will ask you why you wear the clothes of mourning. You will tell them that you are mourning the loss of two gods on Earth. When they ask who, you will tell them 'Dumuzid and Gishzida.' They will be surprised but will speak in your favor. When they take you through to see the Father of the Heavens, you will be offered the food and drink of death. You must not eat or drink anything that is offered. You may, however, accept any clothing and anoint yourself with oil if it is offered. Do not forget these words of counsel!"

Ilabrat arrived and announced, "I seek Adapa, he who broke the wing of the South Wind!" Adapa stepped forward, and the envoy said, "You will come with me now to answer to Anu for your actions."

They made the long trip to the heavens, and Adapa remembered Ea's counsel. As Ea had foretold, he was met at the gate to Anu's chambers by two gods. They spoke to him after they took in his ragged appearance. "Why do you come to Anu's court in such a state? For whom do you wear your mourning clothes and neglect your appearance," they asked, staring at Adapa.

Adapa answered them as he had been advised. "My Lords! I am mourning the loss of two great gods from the Earth!"

Dumuzid and Gishzida looked at each other in surprise, for they had not heard of any such thing. "Of what gods do you speak?"

Adapa replied with sadness in his voice, "The Great Dumuzid and Gishzida have passed from the Earth, but I remember them in my mourning!"

The guards looked at each other with confusion and surprise. They opened the door and let Adapa pass into the chambers of Anu.

Anu saw Adapa and called out to him, "Adapa! Come to me and tell me why you broke the wings of the South Wind!"

Adapa bowed to the Father of the Gods. "My Lord, Anu! I was in the middle of the sea fishing for a catch to take back to the house of my master, Ea. Everything was calm one moment and then the next, the South Wind blew a mighty gale. My boat was wrecked, and I was cast down among the fishes." Adapa paused and took a deep breath before he finished. This was the part of the story he had been dreading. "I am ashamed to say that in my anger and rage, I cursed the South Wind and broke its wings." Adapa dropped his eyes in shame and waited to hear his punishment. As a priest and sage, he should have been beyond the emotion of anger and certainly beyond the need to act upon it.

Anu studied the man in front of him trying to decide what to do with him. Dumuzid and Gishzida spoke softly to their master. "Why did the Mighty Ea give all of this knowledge to this pitiful human but not give him a light heart? Why give him all of this but withhold the greatest gift of all – immortality? We should help this worthy human and give him the bread and water of eternal life!"

Anu considered their words and told them to offer him the bread and water. Dumuzid and Gishzida hurried to bring Adapa the bread and water of immortality. However, no matter how much they coaxed and cajoled, Adapa stoutly refused their offers. They offered him a fine robe to replace his mourning raiment. He accepted and wrapped himself in the garment. They offered him oil, and Adapa anointed himself with it.

Anu watched all of this and was puzzled. "Adapa," he asked his visitor, "why did you not eat and drink? You could have had immortality, life eternal? You turned it away. Why?"

Adapa simply said, "I did as my master, Ea, instructed me to do. He bade me not to eat or drink, and I have not."

Anu dismissed Adapa and told Ilabrat to take him back to Earth.

The final tablet of the story is very badly damaged, and only fragments exist. It appears that Anu is not pleased with Ea for how he interfered with what Anu considered his jurisdiction. There seems to be some interaction between the two, but it is unclear as to what was said or the tone of the discussion. What can be clearly read is that a plague was sent to the Earth in retribution of Adapa's actions. However, the great healer, Ninkarrak, had the power appease it and wipe it from the Earth.

The incomplete conclusion of the tale has frustrated many Mesopotamian scholars and has led to much debate over the motivation behind Ea's actions. One argument states that Ea sought to protect Adapa because he truly thought that Anu would wish him to be punished with death for the injury to the South Wind. Another viewpoint claims that if Adapa gained eternal life, then he would rival Ea for supremacy as the wisest of gods. Without more information, we will never know what was in Ea's heart when he sent his beloved sage to the heavens.

# Chapter 8 The Epic of Etana

Here is another tale of a Sumerian king. Etana's name is listed on the King's List as the King of Kish in the post-flood group. His epitaph names him as a shepherd who transcended heavens and brought together foreign nations. According to the records, he reigned for over 1500 years (though some sources say it was only 635). The most intact copy of the tale came from Ashurbanipal's library in Nineveh and has been dated to around 2200 BCE, during the Akkadian king, Sargon's rule.

The city of Kish, about 80 kilometers away from modern-day Baghdad, was founded around 3100 BCE. According to the myth of Etana, the gods built the city of Kish. The Igigi, the minor gods, created and laid the bricks themselves. The city was beautifully crafted and was surrounded by a mighty, impenetrable wall. The Anunnaki, the greatest of gods, sat in counsel over the city. They held a festival of celebration at the birth of the city, but there was no king. There was no scepter made or raised dais. There was no crown, and no one to wear it.

To prevent the town from being invaded while it was vulnerable without a leader, they barred the gates of the city, and the Igigi stood guard over it. Ishtar was dispatched from the heavens to search for a king. She searched the Earth over and found a shepherd who was worthy of the title. She brought him back to the new city of Kish and presented him to Enlil.

Enlil judged the shepherd, Etana, to be worthy and fashioned him a scepter and crown. They raised a dais for Etana and gave him rule over the city and country around it. Another celebration ensued, and Etana's kingship had begun!

Etana was a good leader for the people of Kish. He built temples for the gods and a shrine to the Wise Adad, who by this point had been exalted by the people to a god with a very devout following. Etana was well loved by his people, but he was plagued by the worry of not having an heir. His wife,

Muanna, was barren and could not carry a child to term. No matter how they beseeched the gods, no matter how many offerings they left or prayers they uttered, they remained childless. The worry gnawed at Etana, and he worshiped at his shrine to Adad regularly, seeking guidance.

Next to that shrine, grew a large poplar tree. In its branches, an eagle nested, and at the base, a serpent made his den. Day after day, they sat apart since they were natural enemies. One day, Eagle said to Snake, "Why do we sit apart day after day? Why do we not be friends and comrades?"

Snake replied, "We are natural enemies. For us to be comrades would be an abomination to the gods." However, Snake thought about the proposal, for it was quite lonely day after day at the bottom of the poplar tree. He said to Eagle, "If you really want to be friends, we must swear an oath to Shamash that our intentions are pure."

Eagle saw the wisdom in this. "You are right, Snake. Let us take the oath of the Underworld in front of Mighty Shamash! Once we do, we can go to the mountain and hunt!"

They sought out and found Shamash. They spoke their oath, "If I trespass against the word that is set forth in front of Shamash, may he deliver me like a criminal to the executioner! If I surpass the limits of Shamash, may mountain take away her praise, may the weapon that strikes at me find its mark, may the curse of Mighty Shamash trap me!"

Once they swore their oath, they traveled to the high mountains to hunt. They took turns bringing down the game to their tree. Eagle hunted oxen, sheep, and gazelle. He took them and offered them to Snake. Snake ate his fill and then allowed his children to eat as well.

Snake also hunted. He brought back cattle and sheep and other creatures of the earth. He gave them to Eagle who ate until he was sated and then let his children eat. The children of Eagle and Snake thrived and grew large.

Eagle began to have treacherous thoughts. His natural enemy was the snake, and Snake's children were very appetizing. Eagle thought more and more about eating his friend's children, and the more he obsessed about it, the more twisted his thoughts became. In his delusions, he believed he would be rewarded with a seat in heaven if he ate the snake's children.

Eagle's smallest fledgling chick had been blessed with supreme wisdom and could see the nefarious plans in his father's mind. He urged him to rethink his plans. "You cannot eat the serpent children! Think about it, Father! If you do, you'll break your oath. You'll trespass against Shamash, and he will cast his net over you!"

Eagle, however, was past the point of reason. He swooped down from his perch in the tree and raided Snake's den. He ate all of Snake's children.

When the serpent returned from hunting, he threw the meat down into his den and looked around for his children. They were all gone! All that was left was a scrape in the ground from Eagle's talon. Snake knew what had happened. He cried out to Shamash in anguish, "Mighty Shamash, I trusted in you and the oath we made before you! I brought meat for Eagle and what did I find? My nest is empty! He has betrayed me and eaten my children! His nest is still full! We made an oath, and you promised retribution if it was broken! Cast your net around the world so he cannot escape!"

Shamash heard the cries of the serpent and was angered that Eagle had broken his oath. He said to Snake, "Go high on the mountain. There you will find a great ox that I have killed. Crawl into the belly of the beast and lay a trap for Eagle. Birds from all over will come to feast but wait for Eagle. He will be cautious. He will walk around the outside and try to find the trap. Be patient and wait until he digs deep into the guts of the beast looking for the juiciest morsels. When he is well within the beast, spring the trap. Hold him by the wings and cut off his talons. Tear off his wings and pluck out his feathers. Cast him away from you into the bottomless pit. There he will stay and die of hunger!"

Snake followed the sun god's instructions. He burrowed into the ox's guts and waited as birds from all over feasted on the beast. He stayed hidden and worried that Eagle would see the ruse.

In the skies above, Eagle spied the feast laid high on the mountain. He said to his children, "Look below, children! A mighty ox laid out as a feast for us!"

Again, his youngest fledgling tried to offer words of caution. "Do not land, Father! It is a trap set by Shamash. His net encircles the Earth!"

Eagle looked at the birds who were filling their stomachs on the juicy meat. They did not seem afraid and weren't acting like anything was amiss. Cautiously, he landed and walked all around the ox. He could see no sign of a trap. Disregarding his son's words, he began to help himself to the meat. Gradually, he made his way deeper and deeper into the carcass, seeking out the juiciest morsels. He was thoroughly enjoying his meal when the serpent sprang at him, grabbing him by the wings.

As he tore at Eagle's brilliant wings and feathers, the serpent shrieked, "You invaded my home! You killed my children!"

Eagle cried out to his erstwhile friend, "Show mercy! If you let me go, I'll give you a king's ransom as a reward!"

Snake laughed as he cut off Eagle's talons. "And go against the wishes of Shamash? I would have your punishment become my own! No, you will be punished as fitting an oathbreaker!"

Snake cast Eagle into the bottomless pit and left him there to starve.

Eagle, pitiful and wretched without his wings or beautiful plumage, wallowed in misery in the pit. He cried out every day to Shamash as the sun god traveled across the sky. "Great Shamash! Show mercy! Do not abandon me to this pit! If you let me go, I will carry your name across all eternity!"

119

Shamash looked at Eagle with disgust. "You broke your sacred oath! You are lower than vermin. You are revolting to look upon. You did an unspeakable thing!"

Eventually, Eagle wore Shamash down with his cries. Shamash called down to him, "I will send a man. He may be able to help you!"

While Eagle had been beseeching Shamash for mercy, Etana had been praying for a miracle. His wife had had a dream. She had been shown a magic plant that could grant life. With the plant, she would be able to carry a child. Etana had searched and searched, but he could not find the plant. He raised his voice to Shamash every day as he traveled across the sky. "Great and Mighty Shamash! Hear my plea! I have shared my best sheep with you. I have drained the blood of my lambs in honor of the Underworld. I have given offerings and honored the gods. Please, show me the plant of birth. Reveal to me where to find it so this burden can be lifted from my shoulders, and I can have an heir!"

Shamash was moved by Etana's pleas. He was a good king and had honored the gods. He spoke to the King of Kish. "Etana, King of Kish, seek you a pit that holds an eagle. The eagle will show you where to find the plant of birth."

Etana was rapturous with joy and set out immediately to find the pit that held the eagle. He searched and searched and finally found the pit with an eagle in its depths. Eagle saw the king and cried out, "I know you, oh King of Kish! You are the great Etana! Save me from this pit, and I will carry your name across all eternity!"

Etana regarded the Eagle in the pit and answered him. "I do not need my name carried for eternity. I desire an heir and need the plant of birth to make that happen. I will free you from the pit only if you swear to take me to the plant! From the moment you are free from the pit, we will search from sun-up to sundown without rest until we find the plant. Swear this to me!"

Eagle swore it, and Etana threw water and meat down to Eagle. Eagle was in bad shape, and it took months of feeding and rest for him to be able to claw his way out of the pit. At first, he was only able to flap and flop about like the youngest chick. Finally, after eight months, he was able to fly.

"Thank you, my friend," Eagle said to Etana once he was fully healed. "Now, let us go forth as friends and find the plant of birth."

That night, a dream visited Etana. He dreamed of the goddess Ishtar, who had chosen him to be king all those many years ago. She sat on her heavenly throne with lions at her sides. In her hands, she held the birth plant. When Etana woke, he told Eagle of his dream. Eagle said it showed they must fly to the heavens to find the plant.

"I have never flown so high, but we will try it. Grab hold of me now and let us go," Eagle cried and when Etana was holding tight, launched himself into the air.

His mighty wings beat the air, and he lifted them up, higher and higher. Eagle called out to Etana, "Look how high we are! The earth looks so small. The mountain is nothing but a hill!"

Etana looked and became afraid, but he clung resolutely to Eagle's feathers. Eagle rose higher and higher in the air. Soon, they were three leagues above the earth. "Look Etana! The mountain is an anthill!"

Etana looked, and his fear overcame him. His grip slipped, and he dropped away from Eagle. Eagle dove and caught him between his mighty wings. Etana was too frightened to stay on. "Let me go back to my city," he cried as his grip slipped again.

Eagle caught Etana again but could not hold him. Pulling his wings in tight to his body, Eagle plummeted toward the earth and caught Etana a mere three cubits before he met the ground. Still fueled by plenty of momentum, Etana and Eagle crashed into the earth in a flurry of dirt and feathers.

Defeated and more than a little shaken and battered, Eagle and Etana returned to Kish empty-handed. Etana tried to resume his kingly activities, but dreams stole his rest. He saw his kingdom withering and starving. He saw plagues and droughts visited upon his people. He knew it was all because he did not have an heir. Muanna had dreams as well. She was visited by Ishtar over and over again, showing her the birth plant waiting to be retrieved from her heavenly throne. It soon was obvious, Eagle and Etana were going to attempt to fly to heaven, again.

Etana plucked up his courage and grabbed hold of Eagle. He and Eagle launched into the sky. The bird's wings beat the air. They rose steadily into the air. Higher and higher they flew. Etana hung on with every ounce of strength he had and did not let go even as the mountains became like anthills below them. Finally, they flew to heaven.

Etana's visit to heaven and Ishtar's court has unfortunately not been found to date. However, there is some evidence that they paid homage to the multiple gods of Heaven as they journeyed to Ishtar's throne. Etana did have a son, Balih, so we can assume that he reached Ishtar and retrieved the plant successfully!

# Chapter 9 The Myth of Anzu

The Myth of Anzu is different than our previous tales because the star of the show is a monster, not a god or king. Anzu is potentially the earthly form of the storm god, Abu, who was a briefly lived minor god in the Sumerian pantheon. The theory states that Abu often manifested himself as a huge thundercloud that had wings like an eagle and a head like a lion that allowed him to roar thunder. For him to walk on Earth, he needed to take a more substantial form and assumed the form of Anzu, a large eagle with a lion's head. Other depictions of Anzu show him as part man and part eagle. Anzu is often cast as the villain or trouble-maker in Sumerian literature, and his origins are traced back to around the 3rd millennia BCE.

The poem begins with praises to Ninurta, one of Enlil's many children. Ninurta was initially associated with farming and healing, but over the millennia he took on more militant properties. He became a great warrior and eventually had a large following of his own. The Assyrian city of Kaluh was dedicated to him, and his temple was adorned with depictions of his epic battles against all kinds of monsters. He basically transformed into the Mesopotamian version of Superman!

Mighty Ninurta, who not only saw that the irrigation ditches flowed full to the cattle pens, lakes, and cities, also was a mighty warrior. He bested the gallu-demons through his tireless onslaught. With his strength, he beat back the Mountain of Stone and bound it tight. His skill with his weapons brought down the terrible Anzu, and he triumphed over the bull-man in the sea! "Ninurta, we praise your strength and your leadership!"

Enlil had sent his sons out to explore the universe. They returned and gathered around their father to report what they had found. They described a mighty and terrible bird. Its beak was like a saw with razor teeth and a crushing grip. Its shouts could shake a mountain. Its wings could create a whirlwind.

Enlil considered Anzu but kept his thoughts to himself. He wondered who had created such a beast for it was not of his loins.

Ea, the wisest of gods, knew what his brother was thinking. He answered him, saying, "Anzu was born of the Earth and issued from the depths of the Apsu. He is a child of the mountains. Bring him to your court. Treat him kindly and let him guard your innermost chambers."

Enlil heeded the counsel of Ea and brought Anzu to his court. He made him the guard of his bathing chamber. Anzu, cunning and observant, watched over Enlil as he bathed. He watched Enlil's routine of taking off his robes and crown. Then, Enlil would remove his signet which contained the Tablet of Destinies.

The Tablet of Destinies was no more and no less than the supreme power of the fates and all the knowledge and principles of civilization. It is the equivalent of what Ishtar stole from Ea and used to gain entrance into the Underworld. It appears that Enlil had imbued this mighty power into an insignia that he always wore on his person, except for when he bathed in the holy waters.

Over time, a thought occurred to Anzu. While his master was bathing, he could steal the signet, and he would be the master of all the gods. He made his plans and waited for the perfect opportunity.

One morning, as Enlil sat soaking in his bath, Anzu struck. He grabbed the signet and was gone before Enlil even understood what was happening. The chamber's radiance dimmed, and Enlil's power drained from him. Enlil sat struck dumb and unable to comprehend what had just happened. The gods rallied around him and tried to decide what to do.

Mighty Anu proclaimed, "Any god who kills Anzu and retrieves the Tablet of Destinies will be known as the greatest among us! Adad, my son, Mighty God of Thunder and Storm, come to me." When Adad came to him, Anu said, "You are a powerful and ferocious warrior. You cannot be beaten. Go and slay

Anzu. You will be king among your brothers! You will have shrines and cult centers across the Earth. We will build a temple for you in Ekur (the mystical center of the Gods, roughly equivalent to Mount Olympus for the Greeks)."

Adad listened to his father's words and considered them. He answered his father, "Who would take on such a fool's errand? The mountain of Anzu cannot be conquered. The beast holds the powers of fate! Our powers are nothing compared to that! With a word, Anzu could turn me into clay! I will not attempt it!"

Anu was disappointed, but he called forth his next son. "Nergal, Mighty God of War and Pestilence, come to me!" When Nergal approached, Anu said to him, "You know no fear! Go and burn Anzu with your fire. It is yours to command, and no one can prevail over it. Burn Anzu and bring back the Tablet of Destinies. You will know no rival to your greatness and temples will rise in your name. You will be known in Ekur as the greatest among us!"

Nergal heard his father's words and considered them. Then, he answered his father, "Why would you send me on such a doomed mission? The evil bird has the Tablet of Destiny. He needs only to think it, and I am turned to clay. His mountain is completely hidden, and no amount of fire will be able to burn him. Nay, Father, I will not do this!" Nergal turned away and left the Assembly.

Next, Anu called the son of Ishtar, Cara, a minor god of war in addition to being Ishtar's beautician. "Cara, you are a mighty warrior. You have never known defeat! Take your weapons and go to the mountain of Anzu. Bring back the Tablet of Destinies! Your name will be sung from the rooftops, and your temples will cover the Earth! We will praise your name for eternity in Ekur!"

Cara heard the words of the Father of the Sky. He thought about them and replied, "This is madness! You would send me to my death! Anzu holds the fates and with a murmur from his lips would turn me into clay! Even if I could find his mountain, I could not conquer it. I beg your forgiveness, Mighty Anu, but I will not do this thing!" Cara bowed and left the Assembly.

Silence reigned in the hall. The gods' hearts were heavy with despair. No one could really blame the warriors for not accepting the challenge, and the situation seemed hopeless. However, Ea, with the sight of the future and wisdom of all things, spoke to Anu with a plan that had been forming in his mind.

"Anu, allow me to take over the search for our champion. I will personally search among the Assembly and find the one who can best the evil Anzu." Anu, without any other better option, readily agreed. The rest of the gods heard the plan, and they rejoiced. If anyone could find a solution to their problem, it was Ea.

Ea told Anu to bring forth the Mother Goddess, Ninmah, and sing praises of her powers. Ea told Anu to instruct the gods to pay her tribute, and then, he would tell her his plan.

Ninmah was brought among the Assembly of Gods. They fell to their knees and praised her powers and recognized her supremacy. Once she had been thus honored, Ea bowed low to her and told her his idea.

"Blessed Ninmah, whom we have called Mami. She who has brought life to each of us. You shall be known as the greatest among us. Call forth your son Ninurta! He shall be our champion, and you shall bless him with your power. Bless Ninurta with your power and show him how to conquer Anzu! Ninurta will be the greatest among us, and his name will be sung for eternity in Ekur! The Earth will be covered in his temples. His name will be praised!"

Ninmah heard the words of Ea, and answered, "Yes, Far-sighted Ea, this will be so! Bring me my son, Ninurta!"

The gods rejoiced that they had a champion and a plan. Ninurta was brought before his mother. He bowed low, and she smiled down at her favorite son.

To the Assembly, Ninmah proclaimed, "I am the Mother Goddess and creator of all life of all the gods! Anzu has set asunder that which I had made perfect. He robbed Enlil and stole our rites! He must pay!" Then she addressed herself to her son, "Ninurta, hear my words! Make ready your army; muster your troops! You will call the winds as you march to the mountain of Anzu. The winds will clip his wings and trap him. Destroy his nest and call down thunder to shake his bones! Set the winds loose and let them whip around him in a whirlwind. Nock your arrow with its poisoned tip, but do not stay still, my son. You must shift and change like a demon of Irkalla! Obscure the bird's vision with fog. Without warning, leap high above him and rain down your arrows. Let the fog clear and bring forth the blinding light of Shamash! Fall upon the beast and kill him, slit his throat. We will watch the winds for his feathers to know of your victory!" The Assembly erupted in cheers at her plan, and she finished her proclamation, "Come from the battlefield to the house of Enlil in Ekur. You shall have kingship there, and shrines will be raised in your name. Your temples will cover the earth, and you shall be known as All-powerful!"

Ninurta heard his mother's words, and his heart was filled with fear. He was no more confident than the other warriors had been at his ability to beat Anzu. However, his destiny had been put in motion and heeded his mother's words. He called his troops and made them ready for war. He called forth the winds and kept them close to his side, ready to strike at his command.

Anzu waited on his mountain and met Ninurta with rage and fury. He bared his teeth and growled down thunder that shook the Earth.

He sneered at the invaders, "I am in command of the rites! I have all the power of the fates in my hands! How dare you challenge me! Why do you even attempt it?"

Ninurta's ire was stirred at Anzu's arrogance. He bellowed out to him, "I am Ninurta, the avenger of the gods! We are the Anunnaki and rightful lords of the Tablet of Destinies!"

Anzu's fury boiled over at Ninurta's bold proclamation. He gathered storm clouds so thick they blotted every bit of light from the sky. He roared thunder into the darkness. Adad from his clouds in the sky echoed him. The armies clashed, and blood flowed in rivers. Death rained from the clouds and lightning sliced through the dark.

Ninurta nocked his arrow and let it fly at Anzu. It did not strike home but changed course as if it had hit an invisible wall.

Anzu mocked Ninurta, "I have sent your arrow back to the reed thicket whence it came. You might as well send your bow back to the tree it was made from and the string back to the ram's gut from which it was crafted. Let your fletching return to the birds whose feathers made it. Your pitiful weapons cannot reach me!" Anzu brandished the Tablet of Destinies, and nary a tip of any blade or arrow came close to his body.

The battlefield went silent, and Ninurta withdrew from the field. He called out to Sharur, messenger to Ea. "Go back to your master and tell him what you have seen here!"

When Sharur reached the Assembly of Gods, he told Ea, "Ninurta has met with disaster! His arrows turn back. No blade can threaten Anzu. Anzu holds the Tablet of Destinies and taunts the mighty Ninurta with it. Ninurta has been defeated and has withdrawn from the field."

Ea heard the message and was quick to dispatch Sharur back with more instructions. He told his messenger, "Repeat to Ninurta these words, 'Do not leave the field of battle. You must press hard for victory. You must wear down Anzu until he is ready to shed his pinions in fatigue. Then, you must strike with a javelin in the wake of your arrows. Cut off his pinion feathers so he cannot fly. He will shout 'Wing to wing' when he sees his damaged wings but hold fast. Do not let panic overtake you! Press your advantage and cut his throat! Then send his feathers back to us on the wind to herald your victory!' Now go and take my message to our champion!"

Sharur made haste back to Ninurta with Ea's message. He shared Ea's instructions, and Ninurta's courage slipped. He was even less sure now that he could best Anzu, but with his mother's words of strength ringing in his ears, he once again recalled his army. He gathered the winds and sent them forth in a mighty tempest.

The battle raged. Ninurta harried Anzu from all sides. The whirlwinds tossed him here and there and weapons threatened him at every turn. The mighty bird grew tired and began to lose his feathers. Ninurta knew it was time to strike. He let fly a volley of arrows and followed it with the throw sticks. Both pinions were cut from Anzu's wings. He let out a mighty bellow when he saw the devastation to his beautiful wings.

Anzu, as Ea said he would, cried out, "Wing to wing," to heal himself. While he was distracted with that, Ninurta's arrow pierced his heart. Ninurta rained down arrows on the beast. Each one found its target, killing Anzu. They slew Anzu's army and let Anzu's feathers ride on the wind back to the Assembly of Gods. Ninurta reclaimed the Tablet of Destinies and sealed his victory.

When the feathers were sighted, a great cry of relief and joy was sent up by the gods. A celebration ensued as they praised Ninurta's name and prowess.

Enlil called his messenger, Birdu, to him. He worried that Ninurta might have thoughts of taking the Tablet of Destinies for his own. The lure of power was indeed great. He said to him, "Go to Ninurta and urge him to return here quickly. Sing his praises and tell him of the glories that await him here. Bring him to me!"

Birdu sought out Ninurta and relayed the message from his master. He urged him to make haste back to the Assembly of Gods. Ninurta received the message and set out at once to return the Tablet of Destinies back to its rightful place.

Ninurta received a hero's welcome. Temples were raised in his honor, and the gods shouted his praises. "Ninurta, you slew the mountain and clipped Anzu's wings! You are the bravest of us all! You cast down your foes and made kneel at Enlil's feet! There was never another as good as you!"

And thus, it was so, Ninurta's name was sung for eternity in Ekur. Temples covered the land in his name. He was known as the mightiest warrior and best among them all.

# Chapter 10 The Theogony of Dunnu

In the Theogony of Dunnu, we return to the concept of creation. The individual city-states throughout the different civilizations in Mesopotamia often created their own versions of different myths, in particular about creation. The creation myths discussed earlier in the book were the most widely accepted across the region. However, in Theogony (the genealogy of gods) of Dunnu, we get a glimpse of a local interpretation of creation.

The myth dates to around 2000 BCE during the time that the city of Dunnu was flourishing and in its prime. The tablets were badly damaged, and the myth is incomplete, most notably lacking a conclusion. Other local myths of creation have also been discovered including the Theogony of Hesiod. These unique interpretations offer another layer of complexity to the mythology of Mesopotamia. It is a tale that to our modern sensibilities seems quite twisted with incest and parricide. However, these themes are not foreign in the ancient texts. The Oedipal undertones throughout the tale remind us that our ancient ancestors lived in violent and turbulent times that our current value system struggles to accept. It also highlights the cycle of creation and destruction as defining themes throughout the history of mankind.

In the Theogony of Dunnu, we begin with the two first entities, Plough and Earth. They formed a union and created a family. They decided to break up the earth into clods and brought forth Sea. From there, Furrows followed and brought forth the God of Cattle. Together, the family raised the city of Dunnu as a refuge and Plough claimed kingship over it.

Earth, whose motivations are not explained, turned her affections to her son, the Cattle God. She said to him, "Come to me and let me love you!" And so, the Cattle God accepted her affections and in turn, killed his father in order to marry his mother, Earth.

The Cattle God also laid claim to the kingship of Dunnu and entombed his father, Plough, within the walls of his beloved city. The Cattle God married his sister, Sea, as well.

The God of Flocks, who was the son of the Cattle God, came to the city and killed his father. He laid claim to the kingship of Dunnu and took Sea, his mother, as a wife. He followed his father's example and entombed the Cattle God with Plough.

Sea then killed Earth, her mother and took her place next to the God of Flocks when he took the kingship of the city.

God of Flocks and Sea had an unknown son (his name has been lost) who married his sister, River. In the same cycle, this unknown progeny killed both of his parents, God of Flocks and Sea. Following with tradition, they were interred with their parents and their parents before them.

As the unknown son claimed the city for himself, his brother, God of Herdsman married his sister, Pasture and Poplar. Together, they made the plants grow and filled the pens with sheep. However, they had to fulfill the requirement of the gods and killed his mother River and his brother, the unknown son of God of Flocks. He laid them to rest in the tomb with the rest of the family.

Herdsman God, following the same pattern of those before him, claimed the kingship of the city. Meanwhile, his son, Haharnum, married his daughter, Belet-seri. As it seems they were required to do, Haharnum slew his father and mother, Herdsman God and Pasture and Poplar. Dutifully, he sent them to dwell in the family tomb.

Haharnum took up the kingship of the city on the sixteenth day of Addar. During Haharnum's rule, his son Hayyashum married his sister (whose name has been lost). Hayyashum took over the rule of the city of Dunnu on New Year's Day. He broke the cycle of violence and did not kill his father or mother. He put him in prison, instead.

The tablet is too badly damaged to go further. In some of the subsequent lines that can be made out, there is a mention of Enlil, Ninurta, and Nusku, an advisor to Enlil. Some scholars theorize that New Year's Day coincides with a breaking of the pattern and points the tradition of new beginnings with each new year. It also is theorized that if the rest of the tablet could be read, we would see how each of the gods of the Mesopotamian pantheon was created.

# Chapter 11 Enki and the Creation of Sickness

This very interesting myth is often compared to the Biblical story of the Garden of Eden and the temptation of Adam and Eve. It is sometimes referred to as the Sumerian Paradise Myth. It was created to explain the seasons and the advent of illness in the world, which can be synonymous with autumn and winter. The Sumerian myth takes place in Dilmun, which is thought to be the modern-day island of Bahrain. It takes place after creation, but before the world was populated with humans.

Dilmun was truly a paradise. It was perfect in every way. Ninmah, the Mother Goddess, had made it her refuge, and it was pure, clean, and right in all things. Everything was in perfect balance. There was no death or sickness. The lamb walked next to the wolf without fear. The land slumbered in the sleep of winter and stasis, not yet stirred to life.

Enki fell in love with Ninmah and went to Dilmun to live with her. They lay together as man and wife. There, they dwelled for a time in harmony and peace. Ninsikilla, the patron goddess of the city of Dilmun, came to her father, Enki, and spoke to him. She said, "What good is a city with no water? You have been so lost in Ninmah's embrace; you have not given my land life-bringing water!"

Enki saw that Ninsikilla's claim was valid. With the assistance of Shamash, he pulled water up from the Apsu and filled the canals and rivers. The wells were filled with sweet water and crops grew plentiful.

Happy with the state of things, Enki went back to Ninmah. Just as he had given life to the land by sending water to Dilmun, he planted life in her womb. Her pregnancy progressed in nine days, fast-forwarding through a month's time each day. She gave birth to a beautiful daughter, Ninsar, goddess of plants and known as Lady Greenery.

Enki's actions of bringing life to both the Earth and his wife set the seasons and the rhythms of the Earth into motion. Ninmah, being the Mother Goddess, was pulled away to breathe life into other parts of the Earth, and Enki was left in Dilmun to take care of the new life there.

In nine short days after her birth, Ninsar matured to a fully-grown woman. She was on the banks of the Euphrates, bathing, when her father, Enki, came upon her while out in his boat. He instructed the captain of his vessel, Isimud, to take him to her. Her beauty was beyond compare, and Enki desired her.

Ninsar, who was also a goddess of sexuality, accepted Enki's advances, and they lay together in the way of man and woman. Ninsar grew heavy with child. In nine days, she gave birth to a daughter, Ninkura, goddess of fertility and known as Lady Pasture. Like her mother, Ninkura matured to womanhood in nine days.

Ninkura followed in her mother's footsteps and bathed in the river. Enki came upon her, and he seduced her. Her womb was filled with life, and she gave birth nine days later. Ninimma, another daughter of Enki, was brought into the world.

Ninimma, goddess of birth and femininity, proceeded to follow in the same pattern of her mother and grandmother. Enki discovered and seduced her. Of course, she fell pregnant and gave birth nine days later.

Uttu, the Spider Goddess who weaves the threads of life and desire, was born to Ninimma and with her unique nature, would be the one to break the pattern. Uttu received a visit from Ninmah, her great-grandmother, who apparently returned to Dilmun after spreading life across the world. She said to Uttu, "Do not go to the river to bathe. Enki, God of the Water, dwells there. He will certainly try to lie with you if you do. Stay in your house and away from the rivers and canals!"

Uttu followed Ninmah's advice. However, Enki learned of Uttu's existence and was drawn to her. Since she did not come to the water, he decided he would go to her. To soften her disposition to him, he first visited the gardener to gather gifts to take to Uttu.

The gardener was overjoyed to see Enki. He thanked him profusely for the life-giving waters Enki bestowed on his plants. Enki accepted the gratitude and asked the gardener to gather cucumbers, apples, and grapes for him to take to Uttu. Once he had his offerings, he went to Uttu's house.

Uttu answered the knock on her door and saw a stranger standing here. "Who are you," she demanded.

Enki answered, "I am the gardener. I bring you gifts of fruit! See the cucumbers, grapes, and apples. These are all for you!"

Uttu was pleased and eagerly let Enki into her house. Of course, from there it isn't hard to guess what happened! Enki seduced Uttu, who became pregnant. Immediately after conception, she began to feel ill. Realizing she had done the thing she had been warned against, Uttu sought out Ninmah. Ninmah, knowing it was time for the cycle to be broken, wiped the seed from Uttu's womb. Enki's seed was spread along the river banks and became eight new plants.

Some days later, Enki was back out on the water with Isimud. He saw the new plants growing along the river bank. They intrigued him. He had never seen them before. "Isimud, take me over to those plants. I have not decreed their destiny!"

One by one, Isimud cut the plant and gave it to Enki, who promptly ate it. With each one, his desire to consume the next one grew. Once he had eaten them all, he decreed their destiny.

Ninmah discovered that Enki had eaten all the plants that she had created. Angered at his gluttony, she cursed him and left Dilmun in a fury.

Enki immediately fell ill and began to wither away. He called upon the gods, but none could help. The only one who could cure Enki was Ninmah.

As he lay in anguish, a fox slipped in next to his bed. "What will you give me if I find Ninmah, the Mother Goddess, and bring her to you?"

Enki answered without hesitation, "I will make your name known for eternity!"

The fox accepted this and left straight away. Enki was very close to death by the time the fox returned with Ninmah. The other gods were angry with Ninmah for causing Enki such distress, but she understood that the cycle had to be broken. Enki's suffering was because of his own actions. However, she conceded to heal him.

Sitting with Enki's head between her legs, as if she were giving birth to him, she cured his ailments one by one. He had eight different areas that were sapping his life. For each one he named, Ninmah drew out the disease and pain and gave birth to a god of healing.

When Enki's sickness had been taken from him, Ninmah demanded that he decree the destiny of the eight gods born from his ailments. Enki, grateful to be healed and hale, was magnanimous and lavished prosperous destinies upon each of the eight fledgling gods.

Ninmah was pleased, and praises were sung for her and Enki.

This myth was actually one of the most copied of all the myths. It was apparently a common practice myth for scribes perfecting their writing skills. The creation of the seasons through the ongoing cycles of life speaks to spring and the abundance of summer. Enki's illness and decline represent fall going into winter where the world is dormant and seemingly dead. Of course, from the sleep of winter, life begins again with spring, and the cycle begins all over. It's important to view this myth from the viewpoint of nature and not society. It is not a tale of incest or rape. It is about creation and the circle of life!

# Chapter 12 Erra and Ishum

This poem originated around the eighth century BCE in the kingdom of Babylonia. It has a unique flavor in that it is not told from a single viewpoint or narrator. It is told in a didactic manner with Erra as the main character. Erra, who was the Babylonia equivalent of Nergal, was a god of plague and the Underworld. He was also associated with fertility and animals, both wild and domestic. He wielded the power of floods and was the consort of Mami, a fertility goddess- but not the Mother Goddess in previous Sumerian myths. Erra was known to be fickle with violent mood swings and unpredictable behavior.

Ishum and Marduk are also important characters in the poem. Ishum was Erra's chief advisor and minor deity. He could wield fire but was also renowned for his silver tongue and ability to soothe Erra's erratic behavior. Marduk, who we met earlier as the champion and great king of Babylon, has now descended into senility and his city is in danger due to his inability to lead.

We begin with an invocation to Marduk and Ishum. There was fear in the city because Erra was restless and when Erra became restless, he was even more unpredictable than normal.

The people of Babylon speak, "Oh Marduk, King of Land and Creator of All! Firstborn of Mighty Enlil and Shepherd of the Black-headed people! Oh Ishum, trusted advisor and mighty warrior! Hear me now! Mighty Erra, God of War, has been restless and stirring!"

Erra did indeed feel the need to do battle. He whispered to the blades of his weapons, "Coat yourself with poison!" He called to the Seven, the mightiest warriors of all, "Gird your weapons and prepare for battle!" He muttered to Ishum, saying, "You will light the way! You are the vanguard, the torch, the slaughterer!"

Erra rose up from his bed with his spirit restless and excited but feeling tired and weak. He had not slept well and mercifully, deciding to return to the warm embrace of Mami! He bade the Seven back to their homes and put his weapons in the corner. He would stay, for the moment, in the arms of the beautiful Mami.

Ishum now takes up the narrative and tells us about the Seven, who are poised to lay waste to the black-headed people on Erra's command.

Ishum speaks, "The Seven are warriors without parallel! They come from something that is too terrifying to understand! Fear paralyzes anyone who sees them, and their breath is death! No one dares get close to them, but I, Ishum, stand before them and bar the gate!

Anu, Father of the Gods, coupled with Earth and she bore him seven sons. He named them the Seven, and they stood before their father to receive their destiny.

To the first, he said, "You are terror and will spread fear wherever you go. You will have no equal!"

To the second, he said, "You will burn with fire and will scorch your enemies!"

To the third, he said, "You are as powerful as a lion. Any man who lays eyes on you will be crippled with fear!"

To the fourth, he said, "You have the strength of mountains. They will be turned to rubble in your embrace!"

To the fifth, he said, "You are the power of the winds. You can blow across the Earth!"

To the sixth, he said, "You have the power of the floods. Your great deluge will spare none!"

To the seventh, he said, "You are as a serpent. Your venom means death and kills anything that lives!"

And thus, Father Anu created the Seven most terrible and deadly warriors. He gave them to Erra to lead and command. He said to Erra, "Let the Seven be your army. When you seek to destroy, let the Seven lead the way. If the noise of the humans becomes too much, loose the Seven."

Now our narrator becomes the Seven themselves. They, like their leader, are restless for war.

They speak to Erra, "Come Erra! Quit lying in your bed! Are you as feeble as an old man? You sit at home like a babe, helpless and weak! Should we become as you, trembling and scared? You feast upon the food of women. You need to take the field of battle again and feel young and vigorous! Your people will not respect you if you do not! How can they respect a man who fears the campaign and has grown soft in the city?

"The city holds many temptations – we know! The bread is sweet and soft, but it lacks the bite of a campfire loaf. The mead is fine and smooth, but it does not taste as sweet as water from a skin dipped in a stream! Your bed is soft and warm, but the feel of the Earth under your bones is so much better!

"Erra, come with us! Let us make our weapons ring on the field of battle. Let loose your battle cry and watch them all cringe and tremble! Let the Igigi remember your name. Let the Anunnaki bow in terror at your might! Make them all yield to your terrible will.

"Let the mountains shake, and their peaks crumble before you. The lowly will perish outright at your terrible cry! The sea will surge, and the morass of the reeds will be cut off! The beasts themselves will tremble and turn to dust. Let your ancestors raise their voices in your praise!

"Oh, Erra! Hear our cries! Why have you forsaken us? The creatures and beasts hold us in contempt. The world is forgetting us! Be kind to us, creatures of Hell. Heed our words!

"Oh, Erra! Have you not noticed how the humans and beasts clamber to and fro? Do you not hear the noise? The Anunnaki grow tired of it and cannot rest! There are too many beasts on the land, and they overrun the crops! The lion and wolves are out of control gobbling up the livestock! The shepherds cry out to you for relief!

"But you have forgotten us! We have cobwebs on our armor, and our arms are too weak to draw our bows. Our arrows are bent. Our blades are dull and corroded with disuse! Rise, oh Erra! Rise and call us to battle!"

Erra heard the lament of the Seven. His blood was stirred to action, rejuvenated by the Seven's speech.

Speaking to Ishum, he says, "Why are you still sitting here? Didn't you hear the Seven? It is time to take up arms! You are my vanguard – ready yourself and lead the way! The Seven are mighty warriors, but I will not march without you!"

Ishum, who was not as lustful for war as his master, said, "Why do you feel the need to go to war? Why are you plotting against the gods? Why do this evil thing and lay waste to the people?"

Erra, full of excitement for the battle, disregarded Ishum's caution. "Hold your tongue, Ishum! I say who and when we will fight! I am the lion and the Wild Bull of Heaven. I am most fearsome of the gods and am King on land. I am the supreme warrior of the Igigi and the Anunnaki. I am the slayer of beasts, the fire that consumes the thicket of reeds, and the ram that batters the mountain to dust. I roar like thunder and can blast as mightily as the South Wind.

"The other gods, they are all afraid to fight! They are all weak. And these people, who you, Ishum, the great counselor, seek to protect, they do not fear me. They hold contempt in their hearts for the gods and me. They must be punished. I know that Marduk will be angry, and I know that I am breaking

142

his command not to harm the black-headed people. I do not care! They will learn to fear my name again. Marduk will stir against me, and I will vanquish him and his people!"

And so, Erra, heart full of aggression and war, set out to Babylon, the city of the King of Gods (which is Marduk at this point in Babylonian lore). Once there, he headed straight to Esagila, the temple of Marduk and confronted Marduk in his throne room.

Erra said to Marduk, "Why are you hiding in your temple? Why is your crown tarnished and your radiance dimmed?"

Marduk answered Erra, "You think you know so much, Erra! Let me remind you that once I did leave my dwelling. When I did, the balance of heaven and earth was lost. The shaking of the havens dislodged heavenly bodies that I did not fix. The quakes in the Underworld changed the Earth and made it less fertile. The water rose and flooded everything. The beasts did not reproduce, and everything was less than before. So, I built a new house and renewed my image. The great Deluge had sullied everything. I used fire to make my appearance shiny and new. I put on my crown and returned to rule. I was fearsome to look upon. I saw the survivors of the flood. They had seen what had happened, and I thought to destroy them. Instead, I banished the craftsman to the depths, never to return. I hid the sacred tree and gemstone. I could not be as I once was.

"So Erra, you think I should shine with radiance and power? How can I when I had to hide away that which gives me power? How can I retrieve what I banished if whenever I leave my dwelling, the balance between heaven and earth falls apart?

"Tell me, Erra, since you know so much and think that my people deserve to be slaughtered, tell me where the sacred wood and gemstone that would bring back the radiance of my temple is? Where is Ninildum, the divine carpenter with his golden hatchet to shape the wood? What of Kunig-banda, with the sacred hands who fashions all things for gods and man, where is he?

And where is Ninagal, divine metalworker, forger of tools? And what about the seven sages of Ea? They must cleanse my person, but they are sacred fishes in the depths of Apsu. You see, Erra, I cannot make it all be like it once was."

Erra heard the words of Marduk and considered them. "Why don't you retrieve your craftsman and the sacred tree, and I will go and get the gemstone?"

Marduk shook his head. "That will not work! When I leave my dwelling, the floods will come again. The sun will cease to shine, and the winds will rearrange the stars in the heavens. Demons will roam the lands, and the gate of the Underworld will be unbarred! Who can prevent this while I go and regain my craftsman and the tree?"

Erra listened to Marduk's concerns, but he had a plan. "I will reign as sovereign in your stead. I will keep the balance between heaven and earth intact. I will go to heaven and instruct the Igigi and down to the depths of Apsu and tell the Anunnaki. I will take care of any demons who escape, and any ill wind will find itself trussed like a bird ready for the cookpot! Go where you need to, and I will send Anu and Enlil to guard you as you work!"

Marduk took in Erra's plan and found it satisfactory. He left on his mission, and despite Erra's reassurances that he could keep everything in line, the world fell into chaos. The winds roared, the sun didn't shine, the moon didn't rise, and the gods fled to their dwellings.

Ea and the rest of the gods met in assembly and tried to decide what to do. Marduk needed to be restored, that much was clear. However, the craftsmen Marduk sought could never return to Earth. Ea created new craftsmen that could walk on the Earth as replacements, and they began the restoration of Marduk and his crown and throne. The process was long and arduous, but they were making good progress. Erra appointed himself a guard and protector of Marduk during this time, even though he was supposed to be maintaining the balance between heaven and earth. Apparently, Erra never gave it any thought, not caring about the chaos that reigned among the mortals.

Erra, in his self-appointed guard position, was increasingly obnoxious boasting about how awesome Marduk was becoming. He also blocked all entry to Marduk, all the while undermining his power. He plotted on the side of how to destroy Marduk's people and told any of the gods who approached that he would cut them down before they gained access to Marduk.

Ea, always wise and far-sighted, thought about Erra and his behavior. The more he thought about it, the madder he got and vowed that Erra would be humbled for his boastful and arrogant behavior.

Finally, Marduk was restored in full splendor and returned to his temple in Babylon. He ordered all the other gods back to their respective dwellings and set about restoring the balance of heaven and earth. The gods were worried. The stars revealed turmoil and bad omens were approaching. They knew that Erra was not content and worried that he would rise against Marduk. Ishtar told the Assembly of Gods to do nothing. She would go to Erra and speak to him.

It turns out, their concern was justified. Erra, returning to his temple in Cutha, was stewing over the turn of events. Nothing had gone to plan. He had been relegated to guard duty and still hadn't had the chance to fight anybody. The fact that it was all his own choice and design was lost on him. Ishtar spoke to him and urged him to set his aggression aside. He turned her away and vowed that he would fight his war to show his power was as great as Marduk's.

Ishum spoke to Ishtar as she took her leave of his master. "Erra is enraged and will listen to no one. However, he will not go into battle without me as his vanguard. I will not go willingly!" With this small measure of comfort, Ishtar returned to the heavens.

After Ishtar's visit, Erra retreated into his own thoughts. He whipped them into a frenzy of imagined insults that fueled his lust for vengeance. To

145

himself, Erra said, "I will lead my campaign. I will darken the sun and hide the light of the moon. I will silence the thunder and stop up the clouds, making them hold their snow and rain. I will show Marduk and Ea my power!"

Erra slipped further and further into his delusions of grandeur. He muttered to himself of how he would knock down mountains and kill the wild beasts. He obsessed about killing the black-haired people and wiping the face of the earth clean of every single man and beast. The gods were not forgotten in his dark thoughts. He promised to set loose the demons of the Underworld in their temples and reveled in how the people would turn away from their fallen gods. In his mind, Erra considered the anarchy that would ensue in the wake of his devastation. His twisted mind embraced the thoughts of shepherds abandoning their flocks, the words of blasphemy from the people who lost their faith, and the images of the gods on their knees begging for mercy. His madness consumed him.

From his temple, Erra set forth and made his thoughts become deed. Ishum watched with horror and pleaded with Enlil to intervene. Enlil hardened his heart and was not moved to stay the hand of Erra.

Erra, crazed with battle fury and ecstatic with victory, cried to Ishum, "Do you see them, Ishum? Do you see them cower and tremble? Do you see them fear me? Muster the Seven and bring them to me that they might ride by my side!"

Ishum's heart sank in sorrow. Once the Seven were set loose, there would be no hope for mankind or any living thing for that matter. Ishum spoke to his master, though he doubted his words would reach him. "Why have you done this, Erra? Why did you mastermind such an evil plot against the black-headed people?"

Erra replied, "Why do you act ignorant? You know they only understand fear and power! Would you have me talk to them? What good would that do? Marduk has been chased from his temple again and has cast down his crown. He has fled in front of my power! Why do you challenge that?"

Ishum answered, "You are out of control! You are killing everyone and everything! There will be nothing left of the world if you continue!"

Erra was indeed beyond reason. He continued on his warpath until he dominated over the entire universe. As he lorded his power over the gods and the few remaining people, Ishum again tried to cool his master's temper. "How mighty you are! You are the Lord and Master of all the earth, of the sea, of man and beast! You hold holy Esagila, and gods bow to you. You have their fear. In counsel, even Father Anu listens to you, and Enlil hastens to agree. You know that you are mighty! How can you think that they do not respect you?"

The poem switches now to Marduk and his lament for his city.

Marduk cried, "Oh mighty Erra, you who had no fear! See what you have done! See the upset you have caused! You marched into Babylon, my beloved city, with your weapons drawn. They had no leader, so they followed you! They were not warriors, but they drew their weapons and fell one upon another at your command! They destroyed their holy sanctuaries and barred the gates of the city. Under your command, they destroyed themselves! Their blood ran in the streets. Young and old, feeble and strong, they all fought, and they all died!

"My heart breaks for Babylon! The city I tended with such care and love. It was like a gemstone hung about the neck of the heavens. Now, it is dust and ruin!

"But it is not only Babylon that has suffered your wrath. The holy city of Sippar that was spared from the great flood has fallen under your boot. You pulled down the walls and defied the will of Shamash.

"In Uruk, you wreaked havoc, as well. You placed a governor, corrupt and soulless as yourself, in power. He stopped the rites and offerings to Mighty Ishtar. As you knew she would, she punished the city and scoured it clean.

"The army you stirred to anger has torn down the temples and sacked the city of Parsa. Still, they do not stop!"

Ishum takes over the narrative again and once again, attempts to stop his master's rampage.

Ishum said to Erra, "You have turned cities into wastelands and broken the people like reeds. You have silenced their cries. You have set father against son and mother against daughter. You have raised the winds and sent plagues. Floods have come and receded only to have fires roar over the lands in their wake. You have leveled the mountains and filled in the valleys. You have punished the righteous and the wicked alike! You have visited death on sinners and non-sinners alike! Every old man, every suckling babe, every blushing maid, and strapping youth, you have put to death! You have toppled the temples and banished the gods. You are supreme! Is this not enough?"

Ishum's words poured over Erra and stroked his pride like the finest oil. Finally, Erra showed the first signs of relenting. "They will finish what they have begun. They will fight amongst themselves until they all killed each other. Then, the Akkadian will rise and will rule them all! Go now, Ishum and lead the Seven. Finish this!"

And so Ishum, with no other choice, led the Seven into the mountains. There they finished laying waste to what was left of the Earth. They razed cities and mountains to the ground. They killed the wildlife and turned them back to clay. They brought down the hand of death to everything in the sea, swamp, and thicket until there was nothing left.

Once this was done, Erra looked around and was satisfied. The gods of the Igigi and the Anunnaki stared at him in wonder.

Erra spoke to the Assembly of Gods, "Be quiet all of you so you can hear my words! I did without a doubt intend evil in my anger. I wanted to lay waste and create destruction. Like someone who had never planted a garden, I didn't care about the fruit. I laid about me indiscriminately and killed both that which was good and evil. Who knows what would have happened if Ishum had not been there to soothe my ire!"

Ishum spoke to Erra, saying, "Hush, now Erra and listen to me. This is all true but stay calm. Let us serve you. No one can stand against you in your anger."

Erra was pleased by these words, and his features glowed with pleasure. He returned to his home in Cutha and gave instructions to Ishum about how to set the world to rights.

He said to his trusted advisor, "Let the people prosper again. Let their numbers once again swell and let them thrive. You shall bring back the gods and soothe the anger from them. Let the people rebuild their temples and cities. Let them raise their voices in praise to their gods that they will once again rain down their blessings. Let everyone help reinstate the mighty city of Babylon, and the holy Esagila shall be radiant once again!"

Oh, praise be to the Great Erra and Ishum!

The poem ends with a prayer to Erra:

*"For those who observe this poem, may the blessing flow*

*For those who ignore it, may they never smell the sweet incense*

*Let any king who sings my praises be ruler over all*

*Let the prince who praises my valor have no rival*

*Let the singer who sings praises to me be saved from the plague*

*And let his performance please the king*

*Let the scribe who honors me be protected among his enemies and honored among his countrymen*

*Let the scholars call my name, and I will pull back the veil and grant them knowledge*

*Let any house where this tablet resides be safe from the wrath of Erra and the Seven*

*Let that house too be safe from pestilence*

*Let this poem endure for time and all eternity*

*Let these words echo across the land and praise be to my name!"*

# Conclusion

Mesopotamian mythology with its multiple civilizations and intricate, overlapping pantheons can be overwhelming. Hopefully, reading them in story form made them easier to enjoy! What amazing insights these stories give about these ancient people and their lives. These ancestors of our ancestors lived, loved, and died in a harsh, unforgiving environment. Their beliefs in their gods fueled every action of their day. Everything was weighed against the gods' reactions and was done in hopes of pleasing the gods.

The lore, with its fantastic details and epic heroes, gave structure to a people whose day-to-day existence was never comfortable. For millennia, these people thrived and made incredible strides in forming communities and cities. As they grew, they traded knowledge along with goods and services, creating a complex and diverse mythology. We are so fortunate their development included a writing system! All these stories and histories would have been lost if it had not been for that one achievement.

Looking at the civilizations that followed the ancient Mesopotamians, the similarities are obvious. The Greek and Roman pantheons echo that of the Mesopotamians. This most ancient region even influenced the Greek and Roman governments, cities, and cultures. The Greeks and Romans, of course, went on to conquer most of the ancient world, sending out reverberations of Mesopotamian culture throughout the world. It is fascinating to trace those reverberations back to see how such an ancient culture influenced early societies. As if ripples from a stone dropped in a pond, the Mesopotamian belief system forged the way for countless cultures and belief structures.

History told through the lore and mythology of a society offers a unique perspective on the society. It highlights the norms and values and brings out details of daily life that more mundane historical summaries often skip over. We must not forget the ancient heroes and their triumphs. Their stories are timeless and precious. We can only hope that one day our future generations will look back on our history and find something just as epic to remember.

Printed in Poland
by Amazon Fulfillment
Poland Sp. z o.o., Wrocław

56068584R00092